NAKED SINGULARITY

NAKED SINGULARITY

BY

VICTORIA N. ALEXANDER

THE PERMANENT PRESS
SAG HARBOR, NY 11963

Library of Congress Cataloging-in-Publication Data

Alexander, Victoria N.
Naked Singularity /by Victoria Alexander
p. cm.
ISBN 1-57962-105-8 alk paper)
1.Fathers and daughters--Fiction. 2. Terminally ill--Fiction.
3. Euthanasia-Fiction.

PS3551.L357714 N35 2002
813'.54--dc21   2001036622
                                                       CIP

Printed in the United States of America

THE PERMANENT PRESS
4170 Noyac Road
Sag Harbor, NY 11963

To Neil, *Mon Époux*

"There's one naked singularity that we all agree existed: the Big Bang. The universe itself." — Dr. John P. Preskill

The big bang is the "primordial *Fiat lux* uttered at the moment when, along with matter, there burst forth from nothing a sea of light and radiation." — Pope Pius XII

I

HE SAT ON the edge, looking at his dangling bare feet. He and Annie had been drifting in the dark lake for hours without speaking. A light on deck gave the mist an ochre glow beyond which they couldn't see. It's chilly, said Annie. The flashlight began to die. He picked it up, jiggled it, and it flickered back on. The batteries are a little weak, he said, looking into the barrel. The light cast a ghastly mask on his face. He smiled sadly. She smiled back. She has my eyes, he thought. He had something to say. But then the flashlight slipped from his hand. He grabbed at it, only to knock it overboard.

Annie ran to the side of the boat. They watched as the light sank incredibly slowly in the murky water. When it was completely gone, Annie continued to believe she could see a phosphorescent trace.

He said, You know what I'm going to do, and I don't want you to do anything to stop me. In an instant, he had jumped and disappeared beneath the water, like the light. Annie screamed, not knowing whether to dive after him, call for help, or do as she was told.

"The look, the sad look he had right before! Did he really want me to let him go? Did he do it just for us?

"I'd been worried about him, I guess," Annie went on, "since I knew he was having those tests done. I had the dream the day after we found out. You know how Dad always said he would kill himself if he ever got really sick."

He had told me, years ago, that he would expect my help. I was ten at the time, and I had promised.

"Let's hope it doesn't happen the way you dreamt," I said.

5

"I know. That look. Afraid for me or for himself. What should we do if he tries something like that?" asked Annie.

"Stop him. It's too sad."

"I wanted to, but I didn't in my dream. He told me not to. And it's hard to know what he really wants."

"I wouldn't want him to have to do it himself," I said. To be at that threshold, knowing that just past it everything you ever thought, did, and loved has no consequence. All value lost. And then to take that step. It's unnatural. "Well," I added finally. "Don't think about it for now."

During the day, we manage to avoid the thought. And if sounds and shadows in the night, as we watch in our beds, make us fear our mortality, we learn to put them off with pills or induced fatigue.

When I am ninety-eight and I am done, I intend to reread a favorite book, take a long walk alone, get into bed with my husband, fall asleep spooning, and become suddenly senile. After that, I don't want to know.

I don't want to be around for my husband's death either. His ghost would be my palpable sadness. And I won't die without you. Both of us must go, then, at the same time, each believing that the world survives without us. To be loved at the moment of death and to think we leave something behind are our only consolations.

For three years, we knew Dad had a lump in his throat. He had trouble swallowing, and several times a day, he would be possessed by a mad coughing fit that would leave him clutching the furniture for support. The pain that shot through his jaw made him consider taking up heroin. He visited doctors, dentists (for lockjaw), and chiropractors; each found and treated a different cause, but nothing was effective, except painkillers. Then, for a time, his attention was diverted by

6

open-heart surgery, an arterial bypass operation on his neck, and the effects of a mild stroke suffered on the table. But when he recovered, the throat pain returned and seemed to have spread further into his jaw and ears.

Occasionally, he would fall client to some new doctor with a new technique, or in the midst of research for a new technique. Classifieds requesting volunteers caught his attention. Nothing helped.

"If *only* they could identify the problem, that would be the thing. If only I knew what the hell it was," he said.

Of course our first thought had been cancer. He had been smoking a pipe since he was fourteen—in order to appear older, he says, because he was so small as a young man.

The first thing his doctors did was check for a tumor. Nothing was found. So Dad was sent on a wild-goose chase after the cause of his pain. The latest diagnosis had been "Eagle's Syndrome." He called to tell me that the doctors had finally cracked the case.

"The doctor gave a shrug and told me that it was not life-threatening. Don't tell *me* it's not life threatening, I said. I'm in so much pain I want to blow my head off," his voice cracked on the tragicomic note, "me."

Eagle's Syndrome is a rare condition having to do with a fused or overgrown something or other in the jaw area that pinched a nerve and created all sorts of problems throughout the ear and throat area. The symptoms matched his exactly, and he was much relieved to know, finally, what the problem was. I told him he could be proud of having such a distinguished-sounding condition. It seemed to imply a too-lofty perspective on life. I was almost thrilled when I hung up the phone. He was going to get a second opinion, but he was already making plans to have the surgery performed by the leading doctor.

The next day, a second doctor peered down his throat and

recognized a cancerous tumor immediately. He scheduled Dad for emergency surgery the following morning. The polyp he had seen was the size of his pinky-tip, and he was confident he could get it.

Dad called that evening to tell me the bad news. I was in the middle of talking to an elevator repairman who had come just as I was leaving for my aesthetics seminar. I had the building superintendent on the other line when I clicked over to Dad. He sounded horrible. He said he was going in for surgery the following morning.

I assumed he meant the surgery for Eagle's Syndrome. "Great!" I said. Guessing that I was preoccupied, he didn't correct me. The repairman needed the phone to call the office.

The following day, I thought about the tone of his voice and realized there had been more to that call. I tried him at home, got his machine, and left a shaky message saying I hoped the surgery had been a success.

Oh pray god Statistic, your actions each seem so capricious, but the broader future one can almost always predict. Nobody knows his chance of living till tomorrow, and yet the insurance companies can confidently place their bets. And if one should defy the odds, do the almost impossible, they'll predict that too . . . in retrospect.

The phone rang. It was Molly with the news that Dad had cancer. Her voice was stilted by her shame that we had been blind to the obvious, believing instead in exotic conditions and easy cures (herbs and spine realignments). He would have been better off consulting statistics than doctors. Of course he had throat cancer. Of course he did. So caught up were we with his misleading symptoms (the tumor had performed a kind of dodge, pressing on various nerves) that we didn't see it. Even the insurance companies had diagnosed his cancer years before, after a fashion, charging him high premiums as a pipe smoker.

I called him, but got his pretty wife instead. "They went to get the tumor," said Candice, "but found that was just the tip of it, honey. It's all throughout his throat, his voice box, and up into his ears."

II

"*WELL?*"

"*I confess I am responsible for the fact that his heart stopped beating before it would have on its own. But not much before.*"

"*Only a little before? Days? Months? Years? It's not as if murder can be judged quantitatively, a little murder, a lot of murder, practically no murder.*"

"*Well, then, would you have me confess to the quality of murder? It certainly was not an unpremeditated act of violence.*"

"*I didn't think it was unpremeditated.*"

"*My intentions were good, but you're not interested in intentions. You are only interested in effects.*"

"*Oh, but we are interested in your motives. Nobody's accused you of manslaughter. We think you knew exactly what you were doing, and your father did not. That's the problem. You did not have his consent.*"

"*I didn't want it. I didn't want him to give it. I didn't even want him to know. His consent would have saved me, and I wanted to save him.*"

I couldn't help imagining this scene. I didn't want to, and I tried to stop myself. I went for a walk right after hearing the news, though a thunderstorm was threatening. It was a cool afternoon, and I wore a favorite sweater tied around my waist, but it must have fallen off in the street somewhere. I vaguely remember something leaving me. And I also remember two people in the street were looking at me oddly, perhaps trying to tell me that I had dropped something, but I didn't understand and kept walking. The wind sent newspapers scurrying, and puffed-up white plastic bags went like ghosts. Slanted walkers held their hands in front of them to protect their eyes. The light became eerie and gray. After a while I ended up at the harbor where storms are large and theatrical. As I stood there—big cold drops started to plop—I realized I had lost my sweater. Suddenly, I began sobbing.

For the brutal facts I had felt nothing. Turn it into a symbol or a telltale tick, and I weep. I must have a form for my sadness. It must have shape, color, and gesture, or I cannot feel.

The treatment would be severe. There was nothing to be gained in this instance by caution. The first three weeks of chemotherapy began with a maximum dosage and would remain max throughout. This would be followed by six weeks of radiation treatments (twice daily) while the chemo continued.

I was the obvious choice among his three daughters to help Candice drive him back and forth to the clinic. Molly and Annie worked nine to six or seven, but I was only studying for my oral exams and doing my dissertation research, which I could easily enough carry on there.

So then, my heretical book would be written in the Bible Belt under the conditions that had initially provoked it. Maybe it would even be better to work down there. My family is the audience I worried about most anyway—not graduate students, not professors nor scholars nor madmen, but them.

I found a reliable source for articles, and told my husband I would leave him for at least a month.

"Hi Dad," I said meaningfully when I finally got him on the phone.

"Hullo there pumpkin," he said, trying to sound cheerful. "When the doctor told me I had cancer, I said it couldn't have happened at a better time. I just ran out of tobacco."

I couldn't help laughing a little.

"Tomorrow I go in to get fitted up for a chemo port," he continued cheerfully. "You don't have to lie in bed with IVs anymore. Instead they poke a hole above your breast and implant a—I don't know—twist-off cap, I guess. Every day you pull up to the drive-through window and get a fill-up. Pretty convenient, I'll say. Some people elect to leave the port in after the cure; it's so damn useful. Who knows what life-threatening illnesses I may get after this one. A port may come in handy. No more IVs for me. I'll take my kryptonite to go, please."

"I'm glad to hear you're taking your treatment so well."

"They have my full cooperation. I was being examined by Dr. Ricard yesterday afternoon. He inserted a scope down into my throat to have a look at the tumor. Now that would have hurt anyone, and my throat is pretty sore these days, but I didn't even flinch. Dr. Ricard said that I was a very good patient. Normally, he would have to deaden the area first for most patients. He didn't like to do that because the anesthesia tends to affect the appearance of the tumor.

"I said, look doctor, I'm from a generation that listened to authority figures. You may be younger than me, but you're the doctor, and when you say swallow and sit still, I swallow and sit still."

"But the doctor probably does need to know if you're hurting."

"He knows it hurts, hurts like hell. That's why I go to him. As my mother used to say to me when she would put iodine on my scrapes, 'If it hurts just think what it's doing to those germs.' And that's what I gotta think about this tumor. Kill the sucker. I will tell you one thing, though, that I couldn't stand. I had to get fitted for this mask for radiation treatment—radiation begins in two weeks. They get you to lie down on a table. Then they put this wet Styrofoam net over your face. It's thick and heavy, almost suffocating, with hardly a slit for you to breathe through. And then they ask you to lie there without moving till it's dry. They don't tell you how long. I swear, I thought they forgot about me and went to lunch or something. It must have been an hour—my head braced to my shoulders and the brace screwed to the table. The mask started to dry up like Plaster of Paris. You start to get an idea what it's like to be buried alive. Buried is something I never want to be, dead or alive. I said to the technician, when she finally came back, Hey what'd you do? Go for happy hour or what? I've been here for an eternity. I asked her what happens to claustrophobic people. She said some people have to be sedated, but that I was one of the good patients. Oh yeah, I'm just the kind of poor bastard those sadists like to get their hands on. I asked her if she had endured the mask herself. She said no. I said they should make her, as part of her training, to see how it feels.

"But then it serves me right for smoking, I guess," he ended.

III

MY RESPECT FOR him took twenty years to mature. It had been hindered by my mother's unhappiness. My first impression of Dad was just one of pipe scent, but he gathered substance from year to year. I knew him as the mean man who was always at work and who emptied his pockets on the dressing table every night. He was a ghost who left aftershave smells and black plastic combs behind and was the abstract possessor of an off-limits recliner with scratchy upholstery. Then from my mother I learned he was a lover of down-and-outs; a hater of kids and family life; a pipe smoker, sinful pipe smoker, who thought he didn't need religion; who would be sorry, who would repent one day, sayeth the Lord. He was the one who sat around in boxers reading the Sunday paper while we were at church; or the one who, for eight years, kept Mother's beautiful roast or beautiful lamb waiting; a writer of hot checks; alcoholic, bad-tempered Dave, whose only love was chocolate ice cream. A proud Scot, whose own father was an even meaner tyrant and would stab him in the back of the hand with a fork if his table manners weren't perfect. And he would become just like his father, said my mother.

But then I came to know the whistler, who could tell me every tree's Latin name, who sat on the porch evenings smoking spicy pipe tobacco, whiskey flavor, the smell of a man thinking, writing, working. We played chess; we searched through *Encyclopedia Britannica* for answers; we told each other our ideas.

Yes, he could be an ogre, as Mother said, and when his temper flared, it was so violent you could only stand by in disbelief. Young as I was, I never took his outbursts entirely seriously. He seemed like a caricature of rage. Surely no one could really be angry about a telephone, or earrings, or fish. His rage only made me calm and watchful, careful, yes, but feeling in control while he was not. *I* would save him. "And a child shall lead the way," Mother had often said.

One day I joined Dad on the porch.

"Your mother and I," he began mildly, drawing on his pipe, "look at things differently."

He had never spoken about her to me before that I could remember. I was surprised.

He went on: "She's not interested in anything but the Bible." He paused to look into his pipe bowl. "And she thinks I'm going to hell."

So he knew! And did nothing about it! He was damned. He was damned, like Mother said! I couldn't believe we actually knew a person who was really going to hell. He lived in our house. How many other children could say that their fathers were going to hell?

I suggested he become baptized. He very sweetly and tenderly declined. Brave atheist!

But then he added that he didn't think God, if there is a God, would bother to send an okay man like himself to hell. There were different ways of looking at things, and he wasn't saying that my mother was wrong...

Suddenly, you became "you," Dad, not that hated "he." You were still smoky, still short-tempered, still lover of work and book, but you now had feelings and a point of view.

Together we looked at the dry-orange sunset beyond the pond; you were puffing on your pipe as it was dying; then you began to whistle "They Call the Wind Mariah."

Though I no longer believe in an afterlife—much less a heaven or a hell—my fear of death is not without its afterimages. They take the form of unsorted memories, of the picture of a drop of bright red blood against sky blue and the echo of a doctor's mistakenly perceptive words. Of the things left behind that have become useless, lost meaning, and so are horrible. The articles in his cigar box will be especially haunting. (I have always thought of them as his relics, his potential contribution to the Smithsonian.) These will be the shapes fear will take on certain afternoons becoming full of his absence. Instead of ashes, I will have an urn filled with Great-uncle Halperin's diamonds and old medals, tiger's eye cufflinks, my baby teeth that were supposed to have been taken by the tooth fairy; Dad's own rooted wisdom teeth, English coins, Indian coins, a bloodstained North Korean bill, a cameo of his horse-faced mother, Saint Harriet, about whose lack of beauty we were not allowed to speak.

She is long dead and dies again with him. She had loved him deeply, I believe. She called him "Davey," dressed him in sailor suits, let his gorgeous golden curls grow outrageously long. Women loved Davey. Still do. She died young of a brain tumor. (It was not cancer, but the result of a blow to the head years before. She hit the windshield when my grandfather had tried to outrun prohibition police.)

"Your mother thinks your grandfather went to hell," Dad continued. "But *he* was not a nice man. You couldn't have been more than four when it happened. What was it—four years ago?"

"Daddy, I was five. Do you really think he went to hell?"

"According to your mother's church he did. It was a kind of suicide. He tried to cut his wrists, you know honey. Maybe you were too little to remember."

"I remember the bloodstains in the back of the Nova."

"I'm sorry you had to see that. I drove him to the emergency room. He made it through, but then he asked me to bring him a fifth of Scotch. Your grandfather wasn't a drinker.

I remember I walked into the room where we had him—that nursing home you know. He had gotten to be too much for your mother.

"They had his arms tied down," continued Dad, "but he sometimes managed to get the IV out of his arm. With his teeth, probably."

I remembered that the people at the nursing home had made him wear a diaper, nothing else, and he had no sheet to cover himself. He was humiliated. He looked little and skinny. I brought him a rosary that I had found in the schoolyard, but he wouldn't take it. It lay on the sheet near his bony knee unregarded. Then I laced the beads around his limp fingers. He looked at me, at his hand, twitched, and the beads slid to the floor.

She too? he must have thought. *Like her mother. Won't they leave me alone? I've lived too long and know too much to have patience for a child's or a woman's faith . . . a beautiful woman and child.* He looked at me, finally accepting my concern, disgustingly misplaced though it was, and made a half-crooked smile.

I knew I was responsible for his soul, but still I couldn't bring myself to force my religion on him, not even to save my own soul. I didn't want to insult him. Surely it was disrespectful to tell one's grandfather he was damned and would burn in the fires of hell.

I had to choose between God and my grandfather's dignity. I let the beads lie on the floor.

He was a hard man. He had cut his own wrists (my own ache when I think of it), and he was not afraid of damnation. This was a man tough as a root, dry and twisted, embedded in rock.

At home later, on my knees, I would try to persuade God with logic that what I had done was not wrong, but I felt He never was convinced.

"I tried to give Grandfather a rosary that I'd found," I reminded my father. "But he didn't want it so I didn't push it."

"Well, that's a nice gesture, sweetie, but it wasn't what he needed. *I* tried to give him what he said he wanted. On his last night, when I walked in the room suddenly a bunch of bells and whistles went off and a nurse came in, beat Pop's chest, and left again. I asked what that was all about, and the doctor said that his heart had stopped, and they got it back up again, and that that had happened four or five times already. I asked the doctor why they had to restart his heart when he didn't want it. The doctor said he had a fair chance of recovery. However, with an order from the family, he could recommend 'no heroic measures,' as he put it."

It's not heroic, I suppose, to let someone die.

"Pop was awake enough to finish the bottle with me," my father continued. "He couldn't talk, but it was obvious. He'd tried to slit his wrists for christssake. I left him at around ten PM, and at two AM I got the call that his heart had finally stopped for good. No one was made a hero."

Grandfather was a difficult man to love. My father did what his expected of him. Should I have surprised my father? been a hero instead?

We, of course, want to be heroic. Dad would like his daughters to be heroes. He does not want us to give up if there is still hope. Grandfather's condition was not necessarily terminal, and there were many things left undone, unsaid, unsatisfied in his life. That's why, I think, my father regretted what he did for his father.

But one can believe instead that Grandfather's condition *was* terminal, despite what the doctors said. He was a mortal human being, a man who would not be satisfied. Dad let Grandfather die unhappy because he believed there was no way for him to die otherwise.

I can arrange it so that my father dies happy.

But if I stand by watching him die, will I not look like him, letting his father die? And won't this make him sad, dying while his unheroic daughter looks on?

It was summer, 1970. We three girls were dressed in stiff dark clothes. The Texas sun was hot. Mother had been unable to locate a proper black dress for me, and I had to do with one that was pretty much navy in the sun. So from the outset, as we climbed into the family Nova, I was a disrespecter of tradition.

The funeral home was a stark pale brick one-story structure with something acrid and unwholesome about it, as if it had emerged from a salt lake. It was located on the fringe of an industrial park near the expressway and the railroad, a fair distance from homes where people slept and ate and didn't think about death on a daily basis. The potted evergreens on either side of the plate glass doors were plastic. The doors themselves were covered in reflective sun proofing. One could not see in; instead, one saw the reflected sky into which birds might fly and break their necks.

I looked at my own reflection in it now. Not only was my navy dress inappropriate, but also my shoes were of a different blue. Mother told me it didn't matter. The need to respect the dead was disappearing by degrees.

A dishonest funeral director and his histrionic wife hugged and kissed us. Her eyes streamed. She seemed to be taking the whole thing much worse than I. She and her husband wore beautifully pressed black suits that had not a hint of navy, not even in the bright sun. The propriety of her dress seemed out of sorts with her show of unbridled sorrow. But you liked her mourning all the same. Someone had to cry.

Some of the staff had been called in "to swell the crowd," my father noted. Other than my parents', my sisters', and mine, there was only one other name in the visitor's registry, that of the mailman, whom, great surprise to us, Grandfather must have befriended on the sly.

We were led into a small room without a window. I saw a profile in a coffin. It didn't seem to be Grandfather but his unconvincing double. Perfect likeness, immediately unlike him. As human as ceramic. The word "stiff" came to mind. *The body is a thing. A man dies, and that is all of him. All that he ever was was in his movements.* I didn't go any nearer: to do so would have been merely to satisfy my morbid curiosity about that Grandfather thing in the box.

Dad was making Annie and Molly each approach the coffin to say goodbye. I slipped into a chair in the corner and looked at my bright blue shoes. *It didn't matter.*

Annie and Molly seemed willing to perform the ritual. They were older. They probably knew better. They weren't feeling what I was feeling. We had come into the room for the purpose of saying goodbye to Grandfather, and although it turned out that the thing in the box wasn't really Grandfather, they were going to go through with it as planned. Dad called me over. "Say goodbye, honey." He lifted me up, holding me around the waist. My dress got all bunched up; my feet dangled. He had held me aloft like that at the sideshow too, to get a better look at the Snake Lady, who had also lain in a narrow box.

Grandfather's face was even grayer than before. His left hand lacked two fingers from a factory accident. Alive he tended to hide it in his pocket or in the folds of his robe. The mortician had it pressed to his breast. "What about the fingers? Shouldn't they go with him? Tell them we forgot to put in the fingers."

The fingers were long gone, Dad explained.

"He probably kept them in a cigar box. He wouldn't throw them away."

Dad admitted that someone probably had.

If you don't need to bury all of it, why bother to bury part of it?

"Say goodbye, Hali. You're getting heavy. Touch him."

I could not disobey, though I thought it was the kind of thing a smart-ass kid would do on a dare, and here was Dad telling me to do it.

I touched his hand. I was prepared for the hardness, that one could see, but not for the chill. He was as cold as a Popsicle. He must have come straight from the freezer. I couldn't believe it and jerked back.

"Please God, save his soul," I said. I went home feeling like a fraud, worse than the funeral director's wife. I had pretended in front of God. I no longer believed that dead humans were different from dead frogs. We all got stiff. Unpersoned.

And there was my mother's Christian contempt for the body. A shell if without a soul. Equipped, it had been God's temple.

How quickly the temple loses its charm. I no longer felt compelled to believe there had ever been a soul in Grandfather.

On the way home Dad complained, "Why do I have to buy a box if they're going to burn it? Can't they reuse it? I'd like to see if I could rent one. And why the heck does the box have to come with fancy hardware? That doesn't burn."

He suspected the funeral directors didn't really cremate coffins with the body. They probably sold the same damned box over and over. Why not? Dad wanted to hear those brass handles rattling around in the ashes. "When I go, honey, promise me you'll put me out with the trash."

*   *   *

As I walk past the living room I overhear Uncle Scott urging Candice to let him buy an urn for you, Dad. I run to your office where Annie grabs me, holds me while I scream. "I want a cardboard box. I want a fucking cardboard box."

IV

PENNY FOR YOUR thoughts? you used to ask.

But I have always been a little afraid to tell you what I'm thinking because I might be wrong.

When I used to crawl into bed with you and Mother, I told you it was just nightmares, but I lied. I wasn't sleeping. I couldn't sleep for thinking. I had asked you what water was made of, and you had said molecules, and I had asked you what molecules were made of, and you said atoms. I had asked you what atoms were made of, and you said electrons and a nucleus, "and that's as far as it goes. You can't divide it any more." You seemed unhappy with your answer, and I didn't believe it, and I kept myself up at night trying to understand how something that took up space could be indivisible. I would slice the tiny thing in my mind, again, again, again. Something was always still there. I found a little relief when I finally imagined that my slicer was thicker than the thing to be sliced. This was like taking refuge in ignorance.

And still a harder problem remained. Whenever I thought of the words, "In the Beginning . . . ." my head began to swim.

"What happened before that?"

"The Big Bang was the beginning."

"What was God doing before that?"

"Hali, I don't know. Nobody does, honey," you said. "Ask your mother."

About difficult things, Mother always said God would explain it all on judgment day, and I temporarily accepted the concept of mystery in order to sleep.

Your last metaphor for God was the Singularity. For a time He reigned there in the exile of Firsts, but when horsed men approached, the guards Newton had lent him fell away. Now

22

He exists only in hopeful minds, a precious secret, like a Jew behind a wall in a decent German's house.

Even with all your disrespect for organized religion, you said you thought there must be something. Your belief had been edited and modernized to fit the presently known facts. Such adjustments are usually made with minimal friction from one generation to the next. But, Dad, I was suckled on what even you cannot swallow.

1927 was the year of your birth and of uncertainty. But by the time Heisenberg's principle began to filter down to the layman, where were you? Already full of God and Figurehead, sailing toy ships in the Santa Fe River, where knowledge was physically certain and battles were fought for Truth.

Heisenberg was too late for you. When you come upon the indeterminate scene, even you believe you smell a whiff of Someone's desire. Even you find his hand in strange coincidences. And you do not object when science stops respectfully at the edge of time and points to the abyss of human stupidity, humbles our pride, and supplies what little faith in God you have.

For me, the inexplicable does not need to be personified. I am content with art, love, and agency.

V

YOU CAN PURSUE any end you can imagine. Mon époux.
*Imagine this. Imagine me and you and everything that never
will be in this world. We knew it would be impossible, but you
wanted to try. No tragedy without ideals, you said. No art
without the struggle to want to be alive.*

*I know. I know, but here in bed I thought we'd agreed to
make believe. Now I'm frightened by our encyclopedic imagi-
nations and taste for the fatal.*

"Candice says you're coming down. Seth coming too?"
  "No, he'd like to," I said. "But we can't both leave."
  "Won't he mind your coming on your own, leaving him to
fend for himself like that?"

Funny how Dad and I had been skeptical of the idea of my
marrying, anyone, ever. Then I called him to say I had just
married (thirty minutes before) someone named Seth.
  "Married? I hope your creative juices don't dry up. What
does he do?"
  "He's an artist, a painter."
  "That's not so bad, I guess. You going to live in his garret
and starve?"
  "We're not starving, Dad."
  "What do his parents do?"
  "His mother died young, He has a younger brother named
William lives alone in the family house in Bridgehampton."
  But he had come to like Seth. In fact, Dad symbolically
surrendered claim by addressing his letters to me in Seth's last
name, though I hadn't taken it. "You've got a good man, don't
blow it," he said to me once when he thought I was starting to
spend too much time working away from home.

It was the day Annie had called me about her dream. I hadn't even finished talking to her yet when the other line rang, and I clicked over to Seth. He was calling from his studio to describe, with uncouth excitement, someone he had just met on the street. She flirted with him, not he with her, but it was a rush.

"Yes, it is. I gave it up when I married you, dear."

"You're so understanding."

"Yes, I do understand."

"It's all innocent."

"I'll forgive you."

He had met her when he picked up the wallet she had dropped in the street while getting out of a cab. She was almost six feet tall. She stooped a little and had a powdered-over masculinity about her that was weird. Her lips were drastically drawn, and she spoke in a false soprano. Nevertheless, she was attractive somehow. He wanted to paint her odd beauty. Lately, he seemed to like to find women very unlike me to paint—women with very strong jaws, large bony hands, and he exaggerated these features even further. It seemed to me that the way he depicted these women was similar to the way his father looked immediately before his death. Seth had probably fallen in love too soon after. But he seemed to be working through it on his own now in his painting.

When we were first married, Seth had painted an emaciated male figure embracing an almost-adolescent female body, or part of a body, for which I had been the model. It was a good painting. Entering our fourth year, Seth's painted image of me settled into unadulterated beauty. Now he pictured me alone on the canvas, being watched by him. Although my body does look a bit undeveloped, and I have grown thinner since our marriage, weighing in these days at ninety-eight pounds, I was growing healthier in the paintings. And where had the edge gone?

It came out in this new collection, in his depiction of these other women. As much as I didn't like to admit it, the new work was better than the work he did using me as a model. It was genius.

I might have provoked it. I had allowed myself to become distracted from my marriage by my work, shutting myself up in my office, declining invitations to parties, encouraging him to go alone or with female friends. He was disappointed that I was not jealous. I should be, because I love him. Maybe as you get older, you change. I don't feel the same now about love as I did when I was in my twenties. I'm more forgiving now, of myself as well as of him. Not tolerant or strictly accepting, but informed, and *not too shocked.*

But this was not the time to call attention to our marriage. I had my books to write, my oral exams, my father's illness. When the dissertation was done, the exams aced, my father healthy, and my morbid fear proved to be a perverse false alarm, then Seth could have his crisis. Not now. Not now.

Her name was April. She was really very interesting.

I interrupted him to try to tell him about Annie's dream.

"I've had worse dreams than that about my father," he said.

I was trying to find a way to tell him about how I believed my father would ask me to help him die, but Seth wouldn't listen, and he continued to tell me about April.

"I just can't get excited about April right now."

He was still talking when I cradled the receiver. I packed a change of clothes, grabbed my keys, and closed the door as the phone started to ring. I was at Grand Central buying a ticket north within a half-hour.

At ten PM I got off at Beacon because a pretty girl did too. On the platform, I dialed information and asked for "Beacon

Taxi." Sure enough, she came back with a number. Unfortunately, when the taxi dispatcher asked my destination, she had never heard of the Beacon Inn. Maybe I've gotten the name wrong then. The Beacon Arms. Hotel Beacon? I finally admitted that I needed a place for the night, and I didn't know where to go.

"You from the City?"

I admitted I was.

She suggested Fishkill.

"That's sounds nice."

In parts, she said. There was a small old section with a good bakery her mother used to own and some hotels not far from that. Twenty minutes.

On the platform there was a drunken man wearing a knife on his belt. I crossed to the other side to wait with an attractive teenaged boy, who was another one who had motivated my exit from the train. I sat next to him on my hatbox. After about three minutes, he cursed his friend for being late. I said, I for one was glad his friend was late. Glad for the company, given the bandito on the other track.

The boy launched into a harangue about the dangers of Beacon. He hated it. None of the local girls knew anything about "conversating." He sometimes went to New York to see things. He loved Edgar Allan Poe and music of all kinds, not just rap. He confessed he wanted to be a writer and asked me what I wanted to be when I grew up.

"A writer," I admitted.

He had figured me for a musician.

"It's a hatbox, not a drum case."

No, he didn't know what had made him think that. My black clothes, maybe.

After a while, his friend's car arrived, throbbing with hip-hop. My friend got in, and then they began to circle the parking lot. I grew a little anxious and hurried toward a group of buildings alongside the track, which, I discovered, included a police station. A cop stood on the gangway, and I joined him, parasitically. He asked me a few questions, didn't like my answers, and then asked, "You a runaway?"

"I'm a writer."

Oh! He could tell me things to put in a novel. Cops knew a different side to people. I wouldn't believe it. He knew. He knew what the human being was capable of.

An old Grand Prix station wagon, which I thought might be my taxi, came creeping along the side I had just left. I ran to catch it, but it was gone. The cop let me into the station. He had never heard of Beacon Taxi, but he found the number in the book and handed me the phone.

The Grand Prix (with "Beacon Taxi" written in marker on the door) returned twenty minutes later with several other passengers. A large couple sat in front. She was equipped with a cell phone, the dispatcher herself. He was the driver. Keep the overhead low.

A big man got out of the back seat to let me in. I climbed in and scooted to the center. On my left, a man was holding a greasy piece of machinery, presumably broken. The other fellow had gone around to the back and rolled into the debris-filled back. Now I was unnecessarily close to the mechanic, so I inched back toward the other's vacated spot. I pretended this taxi ride was no different than the kind I am used to.

Hatbox perched on my lap, we sped through many looping roads, in the direction of Fishkill, I was told. But first we were to make one stop to drop off the mechanic. We entered a narrow dirt road and continued for about a mile or two deep into the boonies. Junkyard dogs were howling.

"So what brings you here?"

"Just a short visit."

28

"I mean, work? family? People don't usually step off the train in Beacon like that. You wouldn't be running away from a jealous boyfriend, would you?"

"Randolph, leave her alone. Here we are, Miss. You'll just switch vehicles."

I got out of the car in the driveway of a dingy clapboard house. When the Grand Prix pulled away, I was left standing in the dark with Randolph who was having troubling remembering where he put the keys to the old four-door parked on the lawn. He carefully laid the machine part on the concrete porch. "I'm gonna wash up a bit and get the keys. You don't mind, do you? I mean, no one's waiting on you, right?"

I shrugged. Randolph went into the house, and its windows lit up. I could see him through the blinds searching for the keys. I could tell he supposed I was watching because he searched with style, as if he were doing it to music. Finally, he snatched them off the top of the TV set and burst through the screen door. "Got 'em."

He unlocked the door for me. "The Best Western, was it?"

"I would have preferred something with a little more charm, but at this point any place with coffee service and clean sheets will do."

"That counts my place out. I could only offer you the coffee."

"Thanks, but no thanks. "

"Lucky thing I have two cars," said Randolph as we pulled onto the highway. "I got this one from the girl up the road who just lost her dad to cancer. Nice, isn't it? They practically gave it away. Actually, he committed suicide."

"That's too bad," I answered, after a while.

"He was an old German guy, always had to control everything. He did it on vacation in Niagara. This is how it happened. His wife and him check into the hotel, he sends her out for sandwiches. She goes to three restaurants before she finds the right one. She gets back. She's standing there in the doorway with a bag of blackened chicken sandwiches with honey mustard and romaine lettuce, not iceberg. She had requested romaine especially because she knew what he liked. It's the little things that matter at that point. Everything he could have done for her did not mean so much to her at that moment as pleasing *him,* bringing him a little something he would like, without ever telling him the trouble she went through to get it.

"She opens the door with her bag of sandwiches in her hand and finds him dead. Shot in the head. No note, nothing. Just shot himself in the head. Goodbye."

I spent three days in a Best Western room with a view to a parking lot, writing to you, Dad. I have been given purpose, but, so I'm told, only as a metaphor. I have a home, but no definite place to go. I've got a beginning, but not an absolute one. I have a name, but it doesn't mean anything, not "victorious," nor "bird," nor "nickelsmith." I don't mind. It's just that expectations take time to forget. We might possibly have the future to look forward to. Who knows? You can almost bet it will be something we never expected nor could ever have imagined. And all from us: you and I (and the others).

I took runs in the foothills, behind the Wal-Mart, where I went for a clean sweat jacket and shorts (boys' section). Finally, I returned home to Seth who was more curious than anything. He had by then talked to Annie and had relieved himself of the thought that it was he who had made me bolt. But he is wrong. I fear I am losing the one thing I care to believe in.

VI

DAD WAS POTTERING around the garden when I arrived to take him to the hospital for his daily treatment. He was not as thin as I had expected, but thinner, yes. And definitely a thin of illness, not of diet and exercise. His potbelly, however, had survived two weeks of chemo. The little soccer ball protruded over his belt, asserting stubborn vitality. It was a camel's hump, reservoir against the shrinking effects of the treatment. It was a sign of his attachment to the world, and his determination to continue in it. (It also might signify a distended liver, but I kept quiet.)

The cancer, though, did show in his face and neck, which was swollen like a bladder. His goitery jowls were red and inflamed. Around his eyes, the flesh had atrophied; the sockets were darkened, making his nose seem all the more large and proud. His collar was unbuttoned, and below his windpipe were two crude crosses, one above the other, drawn on the skin like savage tattoos. The ink probably marked the radiation's point of entry. Beneath the crosses, one supposed, the cancer lay. I tried not to let my eyes fall on his throat when he said in cheerful surprise, "Oh, you're early!" As he turned, he accidentally sprayed my ankles with the garden hose he had been holding. He said he had to get the watering done before the sun got too hot. He had neglected to do it the night before; he'd been too tired.

I didn't offer to help because he told me to go inside and get myself some coffee. In the kitchen he had laid out a cup for me, one that said "Dad" on it, one I had given him twenty years ago. No, twenty-five.

Candice, whom Dad called "my bride," was now in the kitchen getting herself some coffee, still pretty at sixty-three.

Her maiden name had been Frost. Her curly mop was pure snow, eyes blue ice. When she and Dad had married, twenty years before, I realized he was not necessarily the ogre that my mother knew. Now he stayed away from the Scotch, pretty much. To Candice, he was an eccentric, a curmudgeon sometimes, but his temper tantrums were nothing that couldn't be laughed away.

"Let her drive now, Dave."

He ignored her, kept his keys. On our way out the door, Dad looked at the book on quantum cosmology in my hand. "Oh, you won't need that," he said. "They have lots of stuff to read there, *People, Reader's Digest.*"

"Oh, I'll just bring it along anyway."

"Suit yourself."

"Don't let him gab all the way to the hospital now."

My loquacious Dad with cancer of the voice box. What irony. On doctor's orders now he's got to shut up (at this Candice had smiled). *Now maybe she will be able to get a word in edgewise.*

But Dad still talked all the way to the hospital. He even seemed to get nervous in the few silent spans, afraid I wouldn't enjoy my "vacation" if he didn't entertain me. And he had insisted that he drive.

The radio put the temperature at 105° Fahrenheit. We parked the car in the broad blinding heat, the few shaded areas having been claimed. When I opened my door and swung my feet onto the viscous asphalt, the sun whacked me on the crown. I struggled in what seemed like a drugged haze. Dad had already gotten out of the car, slammed his door, and was making his way across the parking lot. I hurried to catch up to him, apologizing. I wasn't accustomed to the early hours and hadn't gotten much sleep.

The sun was so bright my eyes teared. I held my hat aloft to increase the breath of its shadow on my face. It had taken me fifteen years of living in New York to lose that speckled band of Texan freckles across my nose and cheekbones.

Dad reminded me of the time ("when you were little . . . ") we had fried an egg on the pavement. Took thirty-seven seconds. We'd timed it. "That was the year of that long, long drought. You probably don't remember, I did a rain dance in the front yard for the neighbors' amusement. Thing is, it did rain—that very night." He chuckled to himself: funny the luck he always had with his jokes. It was a long time before Mr. and Mrs. Fine would forget that one. He laughed again.

We passed a man who had the same tattoo as my father on his neck and who also wore a nylon chemo bag around his waist. He was shriveled, knotted, and sinewy, perhaps a country minister or the owner of a small-town hardware store, in type very unlike my dad, but when they met each other's look, they acknowledged their fraternity with a nod.

Soon I would start to notice cancer patients in the super-market or in restaurants, especially in the area around the hospital. More people than I would have imagined, prior to all this, walk about with nylon belt-bags like my father's chemo pouch. When I looked closely, as I was now being conditioned to do, I could see the telltale transparent tubing leading from the bag and slipping in between the buttons of the shirtfront. Slightly pinked liquid at the tail end.

"My daughter here is visiting today to see what this chemo treatment stuff is all about, not that she cares for her old man so much. She always had a morbid curiosity."

The Indian doctor was handsome and young. (Dad had mentioned that he would make a good husband for Annie.) He smiled to see Dad. All the nurses and doctors smiled to see Dad.

"And I should probably warn you, doctor, to be on your best professional behavior, because you have here before you one of your own, of sorts. She too is studying to be a doctor, not a medical one, but the other kind, the kind that were doctors way back when you of your ilk were still lathering up beards and wielding styptic pencils. She, this petite beauty—would you believe?—is almost a full-fledged, card-carrying, licensed . . . pumpkin, do they give you people licenses?"

"Only to drive or get married, but not to shoot guns."

He continued, "Doctor of Philosophy."

The chemo doctor smiled at me. "Congratulations. I see your father's mighty proud."

"Proud?! I'm astonished," said Dad. "I didn't think she was smart. I've never understood a word she's said. Never did come to understand her baby talk, then came her secret language with an alphabet made of her own finger and toe prints, then her teen lingo, now her scholarly jargon, but from what I have gathered so far, she is going to *use* side effects as a cure. I'm her first patient.

"I've been listening to her for a while now, and as near as I can tell readers tend to develop a kind of weird paranoia. They start to think simple little words mean every other thing. They find acrostics and crossword puzzles hidden in the Op Ed column. And then there's some kind of problem with hearing. Everything echoes, apparently, and once the sound of a word gets out, it calls and responds ad infinitum. You can never hear 'God' again without thinking 'dog.' I suppose my daughter is going to screw the world up like Uncle Sigmund—there you see? Can't even use a perfectly good figure of speech without showing myself up as a monstrous old man."

"Freud's one of my patients, Dad," I said smiling.

"I would have smoked cigars if it weren't for him."

"What I really do," I said to the doctor, "is I look at people who find that an unintended event happens to be useful, decide it was meant to be."

"My having cancer, for example?"

"Your having cancer, for example," I replied and added sadly, "For example, Mother would say it is your just punishment."

"And you?"

"No."

"You mean I shouldn't hope that something good will come of it?" he asked, trying to restore the former cheerful mood.

"There's no good reason for it or even a direct cause."

He fidgeted and looked out the window. "I don't regret a puff."

Soberly, the doctor removed the empty chemo sack from Dad's pouch, and replaced it. Then Dad unbuttoned his shirt, exposing his narrow chest. A fleshy knob protruded above his clavicle, and the tubing ran out of it. The doctor pulled the needle out of the knob and prepared a fresh one. I turned my head when the doctor punctured the skin.

The radiation center was housed together with the "Gamma Knife" center and the center for mental disorders. We both wondered aloud why. Dad opened the door and led the way. He was more my hospital tour guide than the patient whose care I endeavored to undertake. He said hello, hey there, to everyone we passed. Though he called every other woman "darling," he called the radiation lab technician, who was a stout woman with blonde hair, "Ma'am."

"Morning Ma'am. I'd like you to meet my number three daughter—not that I like her less than the other two. I'm her number one father, isn't that right?"

"The one and only."

"She's already had a tour of the chemo center earlier this morning, but you know how kids are. They want to see everything, can't get enough. So what thrills do you have in store for us today?"

"Same old sideshow. You know the routine."

"Boy do I, and I'm getting to hate it already with six weeks left in the run. You know, that mask is really tight."

"It's tight to keep your head and neck in place. We don't want you to move while that radiation is going on."

"Oh, I'm not moving. No chance in that. It hurts too much."

"Lay down and grab the straps. You know the routine."

"See what I was saying, honey. I have to lie here with this strap under my feet. I have to wrap the ends around my wrists and push with my feet like so to pull my shoulders down and keep them out of the path of the death rays. You'd think they'd figure out a way of getting me in the right position without making me work so hard, but I suppose having patients take part in their own cure is part of the plan around here."

He took his mask and began to fit it to his face. The nose did not even begin to trace the shape of his aquiline beak.

"That's not my nose," he said.

"I'll say it's not."

The technician began to close the fiberglass lid of the space capsule-like radiation bed. "You'll have to leave during the radiation process," she said.

"Sorry honey. I know you're disappointed. Hey, if you wait just outside the door, maybe you will still be able to hear the shrieks."

The technician heaved the lead door closed behind me, and I went to the waiting room. After a while, Dad came out with a heavy red mark across his nosebridge.

As we drove away, he pointed to another area of the hospital. "That was where I used to have to go for physical therapy."

I had forgotten about his stroke that had made his left hand useless. He now held it out for me to examine. It seemed to be operational again, unlike that fumbling claw it had been on my last visit, when his fork had fallen to the floor and he had jumped up in a rage declaring, I need a drink!

"They call it a helping hand," he said. "It won't quite ever be what it was. You can't trust it. In the beginning, if I wanted to use it, I had to really concentrate before it would move, and it would go kind of awkwardly. Now it works better when I don't think. Funny, huh?"

"Pretty automatic actions follow the rather bumbling acts that are intentional."

"Thank you Professor Whoishewhatisit."

"James. William James."

We arrived back home and Dad offered me the keys to his car.

"Say, why don't you call up some old friends? Magdalene still lives near your mother, doesn't she?"

"I haven't even called Magdalene yet since I've been here. Her mother is sick too. Cancer. She takes care of her. I don't think she has much time to spare."

He looked sad. "This can't be much fun for you. Why don't you take the car and go to the museum."

"No, Dad, really I don't mind. I have my books. I'm doing pretty much what I would normally do if I were home, but if you want me to get out of your hair..."

"God dammit!" he shouted suddenly. "I forgot to get the prescription filled."

"I'll get it for you."

"No, I have to sign for the damn thing. I got so damned distracted with our conversations. Candice thinks I can't do this alone."

"I'm sorry."

"Oh, geez. It's not your fault. We'll get it tomorrow."

When I was a child, my friends used to ask, "Why are you afraid of your dad? He's so nice and funny."

It was when I was very young that I knew the worst of his temper, before he quit drinking. "Wake up, Hali. Your father's finally come home, and he has some Valentine presents for you." Molly was already awake and standing in the hall holding Checkers, her limp stuffed dog. "Wake up, Hali. Don't make your father mad. The devil is in him." I swung my feet out from under the warm blankets and touched the cold tile. Now Mother was waking Annie, who was balled up like a squirrel in the twin bed next to mine.

We went groggily down the hall, Mother shepherding us from behind. The house was dark. Father was smiling, sitting by a dim reading light in his chair in the living room. "Where are my girls?!" We approached cautiously.

We sat at his feet Indian-style, our bare legs tucked under our nightgowns. He held up a bag of a hundred paper valentines with lollipops. He gave Molly the first one—"Be Mine"—then Annie—"Have a Heart"—and then me—"Luv Me." He handed them all out, one by one. We forgot our fear. Each time we shrieked for joy because it was so much more than we had expected. Finally, Annie and I had thirty-three in a big pile in our flannel laps. Molly got the last one, and she asked, "Is that all?" because, I felt, it had seemed as if it would go on forever.

He looked at us suspiciously then jumped up, towering ten feet above us. "Is that all? Is that all?" He scooped Molly up. Her body went stiff as she wailed, and he carried her into her room. "You two better watch this," he said. Annie and I obeyed, standing meekly in the hall just outside the door, holding on to each other.

I heard the sound of his belt snap as he hit her five times. I covered my eyes and saw only smoke, darkness, and jets of fire at each scream. But even then I felt sorry for *him* because he had had to get drunk before he could find the courage to say he loved us. His fear of being unloved was worse than ours of being physically hurt. I knew it. We all knew it.

VII

THE FIRST FIVE or so trips to the hospital we stuck to our accustomed roles. He actually drove himself, and I just tagged along. The most difficult thing ahead of me that I could see would be getting his car from him. I was afraid he would feel too vulnerable having to depend on me. He never asked for help, and I wondered whether it was because he thought I was incompetent or because he thought I might not want to give it. Then one afternoon, after he'd had too much radiation, he had to brace himself against the car. He gave in. "You drive." Now I could do something, be of value. (Though there was probably something in my simply being his companion.) That afternoon he also stopped trying to entertain me, and we began to focus on getting him enough to eat.

The fourth week of chemo leveled him. He lost ten pounds immediately and grew grayer. But the next week, he bounced back again, having adapted to the poison like a mutant cockroach, I joked. Poison was now a source of nourishment. He laughed weakly, but couldn't completely agree.

"I'm not really keeping it on. How many calories do you suppose they've got in one of these shakes? I lost the two pounds I gained back last week."

"Could it be water weight?"

"No, no it isn't. I'm not getting enough calories; that's the thing."

Keeping his weight up was Dad's assignment. He took it seriously. Calorie dosage was equal in importance to him as the chemo dosage.

"I'll get you chocolate ice cream."

"For dinner? Then what will I have for dessert? Can't you get me some steak and French fry ice cream? God, I'm so sick of all this sweet stuff."

"Your blender is your friend," we said in unison, mocking a woman we knew, and laughed. There was a woman who was always in the radiation center waiting room whose father had been going through ultimately ineffective treatment for six years. She was very obese, had lost a front tooth, and she believed she was an expert on alternative cures, ways of coping, and keeping one's weight on when swallowing was painful. "Don't forget you always have a blender," she kept saying, as if owning a blender were among one's inalienable human rights. She said, the suggestion might seem disagreeable at first, but there would come a day when Dad would wish for BBQ pork rib puree.

Cancer patients and their families tend to become serious-minded. There is heightened purpose and precision to their gaits and speech. They all have a plan. They know just what to do next. They are going to try everything, but methodically: fuller investigation of the possibilities of shark's cartilage, before turning to the more enlightened approach involving barley green. Suddenly, they are interested in the way things work at the cellular level, or if they are science-minded (even being handy with tools can qualify) they might look into the molecular level of life to see what's to be found there. Peering into that dark forested world, how strangely life-like it seems after all. How animated. Just like our own, only in miniature.

One had always thought that exploring so deeply would wreck the *je ne sais quoi* of life, but if anything it added to it. It turns out this knowledge is not to be feared. It's not like a virus that, without killing you, would leave you unfit for happiness.

Science wasn't so bad after all. Facts were kind of beautiful, at least as far as describing life was concerned. You did find out that death, however, was no longer something you would want to flirt with. It was as inviting as a boring lecture that you have blocked from your memory. Dying would make *you* boring, and eventually you would be blocked from the world's memory. You did not want such a fate. You had thought death would at least be romantic, but now you realize it is nothing to be thankful for—how vacuous, how colorless, how without pity, how without regard for your intentions. It never noticed you while you lived, never bothered to get your name, and couldn't recall a single detail about you if it tried. You are nothing to it but an event without consequence. One of those things that came and went, more like an extinct form of plankton than a man, more like a rude form of life that made an absurd attempt at immortality and died leaving no progeny, adding nothing to the equation of life on Earth.

A kitchen clock chimed the quarters. Acutely aware of my expatriate gracelessness (Texas has never stopped thinking of itself as its own country), I ate baked turban squash and lentils while Candice sat by, smiling in bemused pity. "Are you sure you don't want a *sandwich?*" Not only did I read and say things no one had heard of or cared for, but I ate strange things as well. Don't worry, dear family. I have no plans to convert you.

The table was set with vivid ceramics. Candice loved color. Blue and yellow. Turquoise and pink. She showed off her Mediterranean candlesticks with embarrassed modesty. She knew it was wrong to spend money on "frivolous things" (Dad's words), but they were so *pretty.*

Yes, pretty like you. Complain he probably did, but it must have given him pleasure to hear her squeal in delight at the bazaar in Greece. For candlesticks! On the wall by the phone was a matching hand-decorated sign, "A fisherman lives here with the catch of his life."

While Dad was napping, Candice explained her herb collection. She spun the lazy Susan that stood in the center of the table, piled with jars and bottles.

Point of contact. I shared her faith in exercise, diet, common sense, and, more and more, her hope that nature had already invented a cure for cancer. She had researched new uses for herbs, and I had contributed a juicer to the cause, an enormous engine that made it easier for one to eat, or rather drink, vegetables raw, in which state they are said to possess special healing properties. We had to do something.

"Oh, Hal," she sang, "I just think these herbs might work. There's got to be something in food that helps the body fight tumors. Anyway, they can't hurt. I just don't know what else to do!"

Candice mentioned that the neighbor's mother, who had stomach cancer, had died recently. "Probably died of a morphine overdose," she added gently. She didn't believe in drugs, but it was the right thing to do, she thought, in that particular case. I looked at her. Might this be a subtle hint? No, her bright blue eyes showed no sign of intention. Such actions would not be necessary for her husband. He was going to be cured.

Dad wandered in from his nap with one of my books in his hand. "You left this page-turner by the bed. *A Critique of Reductionism.* Sounds exciting."

"It says the teleologist still has the most important place in the study of human nature."

"The author wouldn't happen to be a teleologist himself, would he?" He leafed through the book and asked, "What do you folks offer the world?"

"Free will," I answered. *By chance, time and space have become evermore narrow, and I have grown a tendency, still warm to the touch, which I call myself. I haven't a god to bless me, but I am free.* "Of sorts," I went on, "found in the fact that there are alternatives whether we consciously choose them or not."

"I thought free will had been outlawed by that pigeon fancier? Didn't he decide we're just organic computers?"

"Skinner couldn't stop people from believing everything is not exactly predetermined. Hope keeps showing up in wistful thoughts like 'The hostess might have given me a better table.'"

"Or 'The first doctor might have seen my tumor.'"

If free will shows itself in the effort to change what is presently and inevitably underway, then you are free, Dad. Enjoy your humanity. But there are some who can't bear the burden. They would rather invoke Fate than to be doomed to ruminate on what might have been. Easier to attribute death to the mysterious purpose of some greater power than think it might have been avoided.

I have often heard you say that a fatal action began when your father had yelled at your mother, Get in the car, and she had obeyed. So even you prefer to blame tyrannical fathers, devils, or other imperative agents than believe that the great can be taken down by some small incompetence or by bad timing.

Dad finished looking at my book and handed it back to me. "I'll wait for the movie," he said.

"What about the book I'm working on now? Will you read it?"

"You know I will, but who else is going to? Do you really think the average redneck is going to like all that intellectual stuff?"

"Oh Dave," interjected Candice. "Hal, I want you to know that your father gave copies of your first book to all his friends."

"None of them understood it."

"A lot of people find philosophy interesting."

"You in your ivory towers. Nobody thinks like you folks do."

44

"Shakespeare liked philosophy," I replied, knowing my father liked Shakespeare.

"Do you really think Shakespeare thought about all those meanings his words supposedly have? I think he was just a guy writing for a living, see, like me. Someone dropped by his desk and said something he thought was funny, and he thought, 'Hell, why not?' and just threw it in."

He lived in a time when everything had a subtext, a something else. The world was rich in significance. He must have seen shades of meanings everywhere. Everyone did.

"There's a new version of *Hamlet* out on video, you know," I said.

Dad was doubtful. "I don't know if I want to sit through the whole thing again, but if you want to rent it I won't mind—if we could just skip to the parts where the ghost jumps around."

And so father and daughter would watch *Hamlet* together. Though I feel sympathy for the child who will not let his father go, I would be the reverse Hamlet. I would pour the poison in my father's ear while he slept in the perfect happiness of his garden, in full possession of his wife, idealized by his child, asleep in his crown, and unaware that vengeful Fortinbras will be King of Denmark no matter what Claudius and Hamlet do because Fate has decreed it.

Hamlet's father's only complaint is that Claudius sent him to purgatory before he could make a confession. But my father doesn't intend to make any deathbed confessions.

When we see the time is getting near, I will slip him a fatal dose of morphine, just after he's had his favorite meal, taken his dog for a walk, reflected deeply on his boyhood, his children, and all his accomplishments. I'll be watching him with a sad smile as he looks around, pats his swollen belly, and decides to sneak one last smoke on his pipe; then after he's fallen asleep under Candice's ice blue eyes, knowing she knew him as well as he knew himself, and *she* loved him, then, then, only exactly then, will I do it.

I won't let him die in the hospital, where the last face he sees might be that of the woman who takes his bedpan. A Kevorkian-style ceremony with forced goodbyes would be equally bad. Rituals are never as full and rich as you want them to be. Funerals and weddings are the worst kind of theater; vows before the priest and public are empty gestures compared to the silent commitment between lovers as they fall asleep entangled.

The TV, located in a remote corner of the house, rarely got the accidental viewer. One went back with purpose. That was good practice. Disdain for the "idiot box" is one of the few prejudices, among his many, I have inherited from my father. We sat in matching recliners, a table lamp between us. He told me I would be more comfortable with my feet up and wouldn't start the tape until I followed his advice. He controlled the remote.

As the previews sped by, muted and fast, we wondered out loud how this director would interpret the play. I said the last soliloquy, in which Hamlet finally resolves to take action, should be read as sadly ironic. But most versions tend to play up the heroism instead. Dad saw my point and had half a mind to agree, but reminded me that heroic was the standard way of seeing it.

We were on equal footing now. But it had been he who had introduced me to Shakespeare, so there was this odd sort of feeling that I was taking over the family business that had gotten along just fine for years without my revolutionary talk.

I told him I had a professor once who said that the "to be or not to be" soliloquy was really a certain form of logical investigation that divides a question into two parts, selects one possibility while dropping the other, then dissects the remaining issue into two positions, selects one of those to carry through, discards the other, and so on. In which case, "to be" is selected, and the option of "not to be," or to die, is not explored. "To suffer the slings and arrows" is then set against the option of taking revenge. So "to take up arms" refers to killing Claudius, not himself.

Dad screwed up his brows and said, "Phooey! I always thought he was contemplating suicide."

"Well, suicide isn't really motivated by the plot."

"Who needs motivation?"

I acquiesced.

He continued, "But he's probably thinking about the danger involved in getting back at his uncle. After all, he does die in the process. Besides, Hamlet is a deep son-of-a-bitch. He's melancholy. That's suicidal. And there's Ophelia and all that."

But most of all, I might have added, his father has died so suddenly, and unnecessarily, before his time.

So *this* student has returned from her Wittenberg University, as it were, with an entirely new set of questions to frame for this old world. Father is fated to meet an untimely death, and this provokes questions about the myth of the supernatural and about love and free will. But it is not with a corrupt uncle with whom she has to deal, but with the father himself. And what does he think of all her highfalutin ideas? "Why does a simple murder/revenge plot turn, in Shakespeare's hands, to a reflection on Man and his place in the universe?"

"Who cares about all that 'place in the universe' stuff? People like fiction for entertainment. Science is as antithetical to art as it is to religion. There are things you will never know."

"You're thinking of *classical* determinism. Everybody hated it because it tried to make God into a mechanic instead of a magician. I have a different kind of science."

Science is not poetry, he said; I was unpoetical.

You don't understand poetry, then, as I do. I believe it is a suggestion that things, which may or may not have any real affinity, do, and then they do. But anyway, you made me cry because I fear you may be partly right, after all.

VIII

BECAUSE OF MY father's membership in the great club of former drunks, in my childhood we had framed in the bathroom (where Dad was sure to read it every morning) a copy of the famous prayer. My mother's favorite line had been "God grant me the patience to accept the things I cannot change." Mine had been "Grant me the power to change the things I can."

I never learned helplessness. As a baby, I did not cry much, I'm told. My father said that I probably lay planning a way to get my next meal instead of screaming my head off in confused discomfort.

I suspect it was my mother's sadness that made me into one who would fix all things. She was unloved, though beautiful. She was generous day and night, and she believed in God and charity and suffering. She never lied, not even about Santa Claus. Neither could she lie about our father.

Whatever precious illusions I may have had about elves or daddies were quickly dispelled. My father drank and had a temper. We couldn't enjoy trips as a family because of the violent way he drove. He couldn't tolerate maps or getting lost. Restaurants were to be avoided. One of us was sure to pick up the wrong fork, or butter a roll with a butter knife. *Etiquette is arbitrary. It cannot be taught without tyranny!*

On their honeymoon they had exchanged life dreams. They'd only known each other two weeks! He went first. Start a local newspaper, write a few novels, run an ad agency. She wanted to adopt all the children of Africa; praise the Lord; live off the fat of the land wearing naught but fig leaves.

When she finished describing her dreams, he said to himself, Oh my god, how is this going to work?

In her confusion, struggling with her self-esteem, she decided it was her perfection that bugged him. So she tried to be even sweeter and more patient, and she was. Sweet as St Sebastian in ecstasy.

Now Candice has come with her bright love, and I can see a good-hearted man with her eyes. My mother's beauty is dark, very proud. She says her beauty cursed her. Candice was more comfortable with her beauty. She was better for him than Marcia, Marouschka, or Marcy.

Though Mother often changes her name, a vein of identity, gold and sometimes green, runs wide and deep throughout. She certainly has the erotic charm of a martyr, which helps her attract the men who say they pity her. But now I can believe it was not her perfect love, or that she kept dinner waiting, nor her sweetness that sent him off to bars and women whom he was under no obligation to love. It was not that, not that at all. In fact, he still cares deeply for her. She had been his wife after all.

I decided to fix things when I was still ignorant and thirteen, that age when you will do the unspeakable, simply because you realize you can. Children can be mean to their parents. No one ever says much about that. The alarms go ringing all over the nation when an adult, who should know better, is cruel or harsh to a child. But what about the child who is cruel to her parent?

Dad mentioned what I had done to him in passing once recently when we were in the waiting room for an unusually long time. Could he still hold it against me? I think he was looking for an apology. I cannot be sorrier than I am, but somehow it seems wrong to ask for forgiveness. I tend to feel that all explanations, defenses, and apologies are shameful. A person should suffer the consequences of everything he or she has done without hoping to be soothed by someone else's understanding. (I am that understanding person for you though, Seth. What do we make of that?) I know Dad would forgive me, and I hope he knows this is why I do not ask.

I feel like I can and should be in control of my life, and that's my trouble—and my strength. I get a lot done, but then I also do much that didn't need to be done or should not have been done.

So the day finally came that I asked my mother why, if she was so unhappy, didn't she divorce Dad? She had tried, according to the rules of her religion, to convert him, and he had refused. She could wash her hands of him. Dad would be happier without us, and we without him.

And so it was settled. She asked for a divorce, and he said, "What a great idea!"

I thought the roof would come down once the divorce was decided. To my horror, we all continued to live together as before. They even continued to sleep in the same bed. I was more terrified of Dad now that he knew our secret, that we didn't love him. But they, as adults, already knew they had no affection for each other, and nothing was changed by voicing it. He would move out at some point, but as far as he was concerned, there wasn't any hurry.

About this time, Molly, who had been married for only a few months, left her husband to live at home again. I had taken over her old room, using it as an office. We decided to share the room for a while until Dad moved out. Then she would take over Dad's office as her bedroom. It had its own entrance, which she wanted now for privacy.

Well, in truth, I was excited about my sister's home-coming. Soon she, Annie, Mother, and I would live like girl-friends. We would rearrange the house. A phone in every room! Music at all hours.

But weeks passed and nothing moved. Then Dad went away for a few days on business.

We moved his filing cabinet aside to make room for Molly's dresser. Then it occurred to me: why not just pack his files into his car? It would save him the trouble. As long as we were moving them around, we might as well.

I think Mother must have said, You can't do that. But indeed I could, physically speaking. And it was done. I hoisted ten heavy boxes into the back of his car.

When Dad came home to find his things packed, he went straight out and rented an unfurnished apartment. He spent the first night on the floor with a towel for a blanket, thinking, *My own little girl packed my stuff. I thought we'd had something.*

Two months later, Mother brought another man (a recent Christian convert) into the house. One night he found me up past my bedtime reading. He told me to turn off the light. I said it wasn't a school night. He slapped me, then grabbed my arm, pulled me, kicking and screaming, through the house and pushed me out the front door, then locked it.

I walked across town barefoot to my father's. He made a place for me on his new sofa.

IX

Now mother was alone again, after a couple of other marriages, which had left her bankrupt. This trip, I was staying with her so that she wouldn't feel emotionally neglected during Dad's illness. "Don't forget to spend time with your mother now," Dad kept insisting woefully. In a way, I preferred Mother's because, deep in my spine, I still feared the original father I never came to know. The one who was too busy for us, the one who smoked and wrote in peace and whom we were loath to disturb. How fair is that fear? Probably not at all. I can even bring myself to imagine now that we did have a special understanding and that he sometimes wanted me to disturb his work out of love, curiosity, anything I might use to draw him out.

The house Mother rents now needs a lot of repair. She has done as much to restore it as ingenuity will allow, but before I moved in, I had to buy a bed to sleep in and a door for the guestroom. The house is worse than the one she and Dad started out in, but a lot like it. Same general neighborhood. Same builder. Same design and floor plan. I hadn't noticed the haunting similarities until I woke up the first morning, not knowing where I was, but sensing I was a child again in the sounds of old Brookline Drive.

I realize that part of my mind is stowed in the Texas scene, in the mustard lichen, a cue for recalling that shriveled winter when I found my first dead bird, and you helped me bury it. I am embedded in the tooth and texture of these stucco walls, so like the walls I first ran my hand along. I am acclimated to this pollen. My memory is encoded in the cicada's song; it instantly recalls long-forgotten nights and nightmares. And the creek willow holds much of what I know about summer afternoons. The pond and the sky. I am inexorably entangled (grown like a web, roots, cancer), too much a part to remove.

I also reacquaint myself now with the bodily form of a certain voice in my head. Startling, hearing myself in my mother. She speaks like a dream, only tenuous connections between her ideas. Her thinking follows the thread of a capricious seamstress, stitching together facts and ideas that are cut from entirely different bolts, made of varied fibers, coincidentally of the same color blue, but one from China, the other from Africa.

All the while Mother is there quietly in the corner, and, I think, probably waiting to talk to me about God. But I am unthinking—gone into mental automation, saving energy for Dad. I can only react with agreeable noises. Back to my insect-like habits.

*   *   *

I must have been three. I was standing at my bedroom window. On the brick sill was a star-shape lichen. It had something to do with the stars out there in the sky. I felt their connection. One made the other. One was the other. They shared the name star. They were the same size.

"But that one is very far away," said my mother. And so it was. "It must be much, much bigger."

And so this star was only starlike, I thought, *and has nothing to do with that star out there, except in my mind where I have put them together. She had led me on with her matching words. Now she tells me they are not the same, that I made it up.* Suddenly I existed. Standing at the dark window, looking at the starmark on the sill, pierced with the realization of error, I was.

But then I also fancied that stars and starthoughts were the same in a certain time and place where one causes the other. What man has joined together, let no one put asunder. I knew things my mother did not. I knew things from the distant past, and every day I realized more. I told her so.

"Sometimes you scare me," she said.

* * *

Dear Seth,

Twice daily visits to the hospital, long hot treks, as the first is ending, the second begins. Today, we parked in the grass to get under a shade tree. You should have seen the grasshoppers that sprang forward in our path. They had legs like chicken bones. The insect volume rises with the temperature, and the nights are every bit as hot as the days.

The heat is a great natural sedative. It's a wonder that letters ever get writ down here. I can't get enough caffeine, though I try.

Don't envy me. I make it romantic with words. It's only hot. And we can't think or love properly in the heat. We're just bored and tired. Physical laws and what-we-think-are-pretty words are just ruts in the path.

I'm tired, and I want to sleep with you. Remember the day I was walking home alone from the train station and you came for me on your motorcycle? That was a cold dark night, and I expected the walk to be miserable. But then there I was in a warm bed with you. It was always like that back then.

I keep looking for you over my shoulder.

Your Hali

X

"HALI! YOU'VE BEEN in Dallas all this time and you didn't call? Is Seth with you?"

"Seth didn't come down this time."

"I can't believe he let you do that. I thought you two were inseparable."

"Lately he's kind of disappeared, Magdalene. I don't know what's happened. I'm sorry I didn't call sooner. I just don't feel like seeing friends this visit. I'm here to take care of my dad. He's told me a hundred times to call you."

"How's he doing? He's got cancer, right?"

"Yeah, I knew you'd understand if I didn't call."

"I haven't seen any old friends in a long time. The girls, my husband, the house, and twice a week, I watch my mother. For two years now. She cannot be alone. She needs constant attention. Agnes takes her for the weekend. Teresa, Katherine, and I divide up the week. I get every third Friday off, but mostly I'm there Tuesday and Friday, all evening and night."

"Good thing your mother had so many kids. But what about your brothers?"

"Well, they really can't sit with her because she needs help—you know—going to the bathroom," she added in embarrassed sing song, "taking a shower."

"You're mother has cancer too, right?"

"She had a mastectomy, and they got most of the tumor, but she couldn't do chemo because she only has one kidney. One treatment almost killed her. She lost the kidney from her diabetes."

"You know Magdalene, you should be careful. Diabetes is genetic. You don't want to do this to your girls."

"Everything she has is genetic—heart disease, cancer. She has Lupus too."

56

I could remember fifteen years ago when Magdalene's mother was having her stomach stapled or popping nitroglycerin pills, my Dad could still boast of never having been in the hospital. Of late, he had had a few operations. But unlike Mrs. Furneaux's, his had been successful. It looked momentarily like he might go for a long time. An altogether new man, he was, with new arteries and lower blood pressure and sensible weight, no longer in danger of stroke or heart attack. He was two for two. Why not three for three?

But, one couldn't help but wonder, if he beat the most likely schemes of Fate, what more terrible and noisome end will the doctors have saved him for?

*   *   *

"I was reading the obituaries," said Dad. "I know it's morbid, but you take an interest in these things when you might be needing your own. What I don't understand is why the cancer obituaries say, *After five years of courageously battling cancer, Joe Blow dropped dead, etc., etc.* What good is courage? Is it more courageous to die or to fight? To die, I would think, but then we don't have a choice, do we? Cowardly or courageous, the dumb soul, noble or not, is as dead as a Sunday afternoon. And if I go screaming and making a scene, what will they write in my obit? Poor fool MacDonald, after two years of ranting and raving, went noisily to his death. After stupidly hoping that he had a coon's chance, he dropped off the face of the earth, just like the doctors all figured he would." He paused. "Who writes obituaries for the scared and the tired? or the pessimistic? or do the papers just shut up about those guys?"

"They make the front page, I suppose."

"I suppose. But where's the dignity in that?" Then he remembered a death he had read about the week before. "Aunt

57

Latina, ninety-two, made the news section. A little senile, but otherwise in the very pink of health, she enters a parking garage, walks to the fifth level and steps over the edge. Family distraught."

"The way the obituaries call the family members 'survivors' is strangely dramatic but right. Couldn't she have waited for her natural end?" I asked. "It couldn't have been far off."

"Well, what's natural for her? I mean, maybe she didn't want her kids to have to fool with her anymore."

"She might have chosen a more serene gesture with which to end her life. The End tends to impose a meaning on everything that goes before. If you know what I mean: the culminating moment."

"And some guys just croak on the john. What interpretation would I want to give my life? If I could choose, I'd go on the porch smoking my pipe, my reason for living, and maybe my reason for dying. There's poetry in that."

So how does one play the part of the hero in today's obit? Hamlet's question. A good question, one without an easy answer. One must be careful lest one's heroism, choosing to die, necessitate someone else's cowardice, standing by. Of course, there is the option of collective sacrifice. The cancer patients and family members who suffer longest and hardest win. The quality of the day doesn't seem to count for as much as the number.

My father has no intention of letting me be a heroic sufferer for his sake. He thinks it's foolishness. For him the pain of his dying will only last minutes. For me, my life.

But if I did hang on to hope to the end, like Magdalene, he would be proud, proud of his daughter for being so irrational.

XI

IT WAS MY turn to pick up the video. He had hinted that he might like a good history. In that section, perhaps incorrectly shelved, was "The History of the Universes." Intending to please him, I was destined to please myself instead, it seemed.

"Humph," he frowned, reading the title and turning the cassette over. "How can there be more than one universe?"

I felt shamed, then I realized his error. "Dad, that's like asking how there can be more than one unicycle."

He looked at me startled, as if I were someone he had taken for a foreigner and I suddenly spoke his own language. "Hey, smart alec. Who taught you everything you know? Or at least paid for some of it? All right. Let's see what we can learn from this."

The show said that there was no beginning, that this universe is but a beat in a cosmic pulse, that its future is closed, decided, and predictable. It starts with the Big Bang and ends with the Big Crunch, then does the whole thing again in reserve. The universe will go on exploding and imploding forever. Life may have had countless false starts, and maybe we are just another dead-end.

I said, "That's the kind of scheme that makes scientists give up their work in favor of religion."

Dad didn't like the Big Crunch idea either. "No one wants to think it'll all just end in nothing," he said.

Idealism may have stunned us momentarily, but we soon recovered. We can't know the thing-in-itself, but that is not a problem because there may *be* no such thing. That we can take. In fact, it's rather nice to believe that we are miraculous beings, almost, in the way that we see unity in disconnected ever-changing parts. With that we can be (or could have been;

the bad news followed too quickly) happy. The problem came when we found we make meaning to no advantage. Not even the human race is immortal. Our galactic home will go cold.

"Maybe it's like Buddhism!" he suddenly realized. "You see, the Big Bang-Big Crunch cycle might be a form of reincarnation!"

"But reincarnation would have to involve some kind of memory, some way of letting the past inform the future. In the Big Crunch, all matter and information would be turned into quark soup."

"That's pretty depressing."

"It's not *my* view. I'm hoping they find the universe is flat, so that it won't collapse."

"Well, I'm not going to wait on the edge of my seat till *they* decide. I'm going to bed."

That night in bed I was restless. I had forgotten what it was like to feel fear so empty, as I had most poignantly at three or four, realizing for the first time that I couldn't understand what it meant to begin or to end.

Outside my window, mockingbirds were swirling around the parklight catching insects. The noises they made. Meaningful noises. *You might call it genius, the way they can sound uncannily like the bells of St. Paul Le Jeune, which they have never heard. A sublime accident, with no more than visceral intention, and no less.*

There was the consolation one needed. I turned, gaining a cooler patch of pillow. I imagined my father awake in his bed too, feeling not just the family edifice crumble, but also the whole world. Grabbing at the cold comfort that there may be other universes to continue if ours should end in the Big Crunch. And wondering why it should make a difference that this one continue. Clearly it does. If not I, then at least my young, my genetically reminiscent self, would go on. If not I, then my children, or someone else's children, or if not humans, then extra-terrestrials, and so on. There was something in that, yes. Or better yet, my contribution might continue in the form of thought, a philosophy more solid than any rock, longer lasting than any Rembrandt, more robust than any old god's dogma.

Why should it matter to me that something survive the Big Crunch or heat death? Why does continuity feel so important? The scaffolding up of good will, so that somehow, someway, progress may come of every human life and the whole business of living be somehow worthwhile.

Continue my work. One wants a bright graduate student to continue one's theories, even change them if necessary so that they work better. Make some use out of them. That's the thing.

Lately, Candice had mentioned, Dad had become interested in selecting out various things that he thought one of his daughters could use. Every time Candice went to throw out an old table or can opener, he would say, "Maybe one of the girls could use that." What really bothered him, I supposed, was the idea that something he had sweated for should go to waste. Our cities and our poems erased.

Dad sat at the breakfast table scratching his head and said, "I'd always kind of thought the Big Bang was what we call God, the beginning, you know, of everything, when he set the universe running. The first and probably only miracle. But who needs more than one?"

"Who needs one?"

"How else do you explain it?"

"The universe gave rise to itself. Even if originally all the fuzzy particles were all mixed up, there is still a chance that in that vague twilight soup, some differences, call them night and day, in some corner somewhere, coincidentally segregated. A kind of selection would have taken over from there."

"Do you really think you can understand what the scientists say?"

"It seems a little easier to understand than a concept like God, which I don't get at all, not even a little bit."

"Don't you think it's comforting?"

"I like their cathedrals, hymns, their golden rule, and some of their art. We could just call God 'Stochastic Resonance,' if we really wanted to hang on to our churches and rituals and such, but we would have to strip Him of His look-ahead and know-all. He would be known only through his statistics. And you could only get a fix on him as he receded into the distance."

Dad sighed. "They'll all decide you're all wrong tomorrow. Look at Ptolemy. Quantum leaps and stuff. Who can believe it? How can they be so certain about uncertainty?"

"Because it works. Newton wasn't even wrong. They just found a limit to how far his physics could be applied."

He took a sip of his coffee and set his cup down angrily. "We should get going, if we want to make my chemo appointment."

XII

A THRESHOLD IS crossed when steam turns to water, or water to
ice, or back again. There is nothing inherent in the molecular
structure of water to suggest ice. To a sultan king, an Eskimo's
world would seem like a fairy tale. Might a similar threshold
be crossed when a spirit turns human, or a human animal, or
back again? There is nothing inherent in my molecular struc-
ture to suggest my soul—some might say with hope. But to
guess what is impossible to predict would be incredibly lucky.
Perhaps there is another form beyond the present state of this
body, but instead of a soul, it will probably be more like steam,
something we never bothered to dream.

I sat with my father in the waiting room, reading an article
on a theory about the origin of life, as he was losing his. *Just*
what is it you're losing, Dad? It cannot be merely the ability
to maintain stasis by changing. Even crystals imperfectly
reproduce themselves in mud.

"Oh see, watch this, pumpkin," he said. "Here comes that
gal. She drops her mother off. Signs her in. She gets her settled
in a chair. Then look. She's got to bolt out to have a smoke.
Look at her puffing away like an addict! Probably spends
forty-five minutes in the car with Mom, driving all the way in
from Longview or some-such-place every day, and she's 'bout
had it. Look at her go."

Through the window I watched the woman who stood
smoking in that contemplative trance that cigarette smoking
seems to demand. (My father's pipe-smoking look had been
querulous.) She exhaled impatiently. God, she was glad to get
outside, hot as it was, for a smoke. Her whole body showed the
fatigue of taking care of her mother, not a special kind of
fatigue from extreme emotional duress, but an ordinary tired-

ness of a long tedious day-on-the-job. The mental duress would come later, or even after. Right now, she was still in shock over the banality of dealing with the death of her own mother, after whom she had taken so, appearance-wise. She ground the butt on the pavement with unnecessary thoroughness and reentered the waiting room like one who had just gone out to scream her head off and was now relieved.

"Mr. MacDonald, we're ready for you now," called the knock-kneed blonde nurse. He followed her down the hall, saluting me goodbye.

Did the smoker's mother ever dream she would have a daughter such as she? No, but in retrospect, she sees how it happened. In retrospect, it seems like her Fate. That is eating at her heart more than the cancer. The helplessness.

My father disappeared around the corner.

Time is working without reason; tritium emits a particle; a universe begins; or water freezes. The as-if-it-were haunts empty space, spongy potential foam infused. There is a hesitation, then the door is shut, the die is cast, the story writ. I once thought God governed these thresholds, and I kept the way cluttered with relics. Now the way is windswept, and reality comes and goes just as well without a keeper.

Ever since Darwin it's looked like riot for tomorrow, but in the rearview mirror all is determined, if not inevitable. I see, reflected there in the past, immigrants from this future void, virtual men of no consequence, now real men of vigor and strength, creating world out of nothing. History is the great creative force, not, as I once thought, mere matter, maker, or form. Things are as they are because they were as they were, more or less. And who knows what will be?

"So if you don't believe in anything supernatural, what do you think happens to us when we die? Do we just decay like a dead flower, and that's it?" asked Dad suddenly on the way back home. *Here is the question we have been dreading.*

"I think we go on in our actions and the ideas we leave behind," I offered feebly.

"What about the soul, or mind, or spirit? You don't believe in any of that?"

I must have seemed mature behind the wheel, coming gently to a stop at the light, signaling before each lane change. *I've become your parent now, Dad. How I hate it. How it feels so false.* "I like to think what we call 'life' isn't a physical thing, but a kind of behavior, a pattern. If you believe this, then you can imagine that you live on even after the body's gone in the things you've done."

"It's that cliché?"

"And when you die maybe others take over where you've left off. Your life may turn into something you never imagined."

"But that wouldn't be me anymore."

"No, no longer just you, but more than you, too." *There must be change.*

We passed an elderly Mexican man with long gray hair, working on a construction site. The day was brutally hot, but he was valiantly working away, sorting through debris. Dad pointed him out.

"What if somebody's ideas don't matter to anybody else?"

"You never know."

"So us old coots, so set in our ways, need to move over so that someone else, who doesn't know nothing, can come along and shake up what I've found to be true and good and right and get something really new out of it, and that'll be progress?"

"There are wonderful things about your own philosophy that you've never dreamt. You're not the same person you were as a child."

"Humanity goes on while the individual gets sloughed off in the shower like any old dead cell? All the better. I know you mean well, sweetie, but I'm not buying it."

Knowing I would just get in the way if I stayed around might make it easier for me to go. If I knew I was no longer limber, had nothing more to add, no more surprises to spring, no more lucky mistakes to make—Oh but Dad you are right. Death of the individual should not, on pain of inconceivability, be construed as a kind of abstract survival for the species, not even for slime mold.

We drove along without speaking for a while. Finally Dad made a comment about another large structure that was being erected on the corner. "I wonder what it's going to be. Another grocery store or church? Damn Baptists."

All the major thoroughfares in suburban North Dallas were dominated by superstores and superchurches.

"I don't especially begrudge them their size or steeple or humongous cross," I said as we drove past a block with four separate congregations in a row. "I just wish they had better taste."

"And interfered less. The church of Mary Kay sold its building on our corner, don't know if I mentioned it. They bought many an acre out in Plano where the cattle fields can absorb their numbers. But it turns out the twenty-story steeple they intend to erect will interfere with the flight patterns of Addison Airport. You know what the bastards did? They hired a team of attorneys to force Air Traffic Control to re-route all flights. Their egomania astounds me."

"I kind of like steeples, symbols of longing. And I don't dislike all religions. Organization is life. Without a little religion we'd have only rubble, and we would eat our meat uncooked and share our spouses, whether they liked it or not...but not so organized." *Or life would become frozen and*

persist without change. Heaven would be beautiful like a
crystal, but not alive.

"Did I ever show you this?" asked Dad. He unfolded his
"wallet," a laminated cascade of photos and business cards,
and he pointed out a yellowed identification card:

> *David MacDonald, Minister*
> *Fifth Church of God*

"Why 'fifth'?" I asked.

"As in fifth of Scotch."

He flipped the card accordion shut, shifted, and stuffed it
back into his back pocket. "Cost me twenty-five dollars. But
it's authentic. With that I can open my own congregation in my
own home, if I wanted. Tax-exempt. Remember when they
decided to build that church out on East Meadow Lane? A
bunch of the neighbors and I sent away to become certified as
ministers. I think Wilcox must have found the ad in the back
of a massage magazine or something. We all went to the city
council meeting and flashed our cards, said that if they let that
damn church go in, we were all going to start our own
churches, and they could just try to collect property taxes. And
we would get every last son-of-a-bitch in the neighborhood—
who wasn't a Baptist—to do the same.

"I'll tell you why we didn't want that church to go in. Not
that I have anything against God, but his faithful behave like
criminals. They use up the quiet and cause traffic problems.
They don't watch for your dogs or kids while they're zooming
back home to drink beer or to get back to fornicating.

"Too bad our plan didn't work. Too many of them. Too many
Mary Kay dollars. Do you know they painted the pews pink?

"But anyway, I found the ministry card the other day.
Noticed it hadn't expired. Good for eternity. And I got to

thinking I might really go ahead and start my own church. Did I ever mention my idea for the Concentric Corporation? It's my semi-serious theory about God, His divine corporate Structure and Circular Infinity."

He had, years and years before. He was going to beat organized religion at its own game. At the time, I had envied and feared for my dad for having the thought, as if he were the Evil Knieval of morality.

"All earthly churches are based on the greatest corporation of all, in heaven. You can tell," he said, "by the way churches manage to make so much damned money without paying taxes like the rest of us poor bastards. I'm with Luther. Some of the financial shenanigans of organized religion get my goat. I got to figuring it was all one big for-profit business, run under the guise of non-profit brotherly and sisterly love. God must be CEO, the saints members of the board, and the angels stockholders. Jesus is Vice-President. And the Holy Ghost?"

"Treasurer?"

"Exactly. You can see how people might start to believe me because it does begin to seem to make sense. Hey, you could be one of the salesministers in charge of mail order. Hell, I bet you could get a million people in California to send you a two-dollar donation. But the best scam is the brokers'. The corporate assets are souls, see. There is a limited supply, and they have to be recycled—reincarnated."

I said the plan reminded me of Jonathan Swift's "Against Abolishing Christianity" in which a naïve atheist, defending religion, inadvertently critiques hypocrisy.

"Be assured I'm not an atheist," he replied. "I figure there must be a God, Buddha, Allah or whatever you choose to call him or her running the show. I'm just not a big fan of organized religion."

* * *

A month after his death, Molly sent me a box containing the papers that were left in his office. I found a file marked "Concentric Corporation," in which Dad collected newspapers articles from 1965-1978 on the Big Bang and life after death. I read many familiar phrases, and I realize he must have mentioned them to me when I was very young. So it was he, after all, who got me interested in cosmology. Most of the articles were pseudo-scientific accounts of a universe that was supernaturally created in the Big Bang. Some argued that reincarnation or some form of life after death could be understood scientifically in terms of the recycling of matter. Some sections he had underlined in blue:

Original 'big-bang': Universe-creating sound reported:
". . . Sir Bernard said sensitive instruments have heard what is believed to be the last of the shattering of the 'primeval fireball' which started its unimaginable expansion 10 billion years ago . . ."

White Holes Seen in Space:
". . . .Whereas black holes are sinks, white holes represent sources out of which material flows into our universe.... Where does that matter originate? One theory states that there are two universes—the one we are in with its matter draining away into black holes, and another anti-universe with its anti-matter draining away into this universe . . . ."

Soul travelers practice ancient religion:
". . . Through spiritual exercises and guidance, says Enkist Mr. Ginn, the soul, or true person, is freed from the physical body and allowed to roam in secret worlds or 'other levels of consciousness.' Souls may have many incarnations, sometimes millions, in order to learn as much as possible about this world . . . ."

Fossil radiation theory:

"... A scientist at the University of California has found some 'fossil' radiation in the world's atmosphere which may tell a lot about how the universe was formed. According to modern cosmological theory, said Richards, the big explosion (what caused it is not known) resulted in protons, electrons, and neutrons flying around each other. Richards became interested in studying the big-bang when in 1965, scientists at Bell Telephone Laboratories unexpectedly discovered radiation. His findings, he believes, further nail down the story of how the world began with a huge explosion 10 billion years ago ... "

In the Beginning, science, the universe, and God:

"... Robert Jastrow, director of NASA's Goddard Institute for Space Studies, is convinced that 'The Big Bang and Biblical accounts of Genesis are the same.' Theologians generally are delighted with the proof that the universe had a beginning, but some scientists are curiously upset. Einstein had well-defined feelings about God, but not as the Creator or Prime Mover. For Einstein, the existence of God was proved by the fact that there is order in the universe. He believed the universe was static and unchanging. Einstein resisted the evidence for an expanding universe and a beginning in time until he was finally forced to accept Hubble's proof in 1930.... Scientists have scaled the mountains of ignorance, they are about to conquer the highest peak; as they pull themselves over the final rock, they are greeted by a band of theologians who have been sitting there for centuries ..."

From Big Bang to Big Crunch:

"... Gravity may not be strong enough to keep the universe from expanding forever. Recent research sheds new light on the key cosmological question about the distant future. In one projection, if the average density of matter in the universe is great enough, the mutual attraction between bodies will eventually slow expansion down to a halt, then contract and finally collapse. It has also been suggested that the universe might begin a new era of expansion with a new Big Bang. In that manner the universe could go on cycling forever . . ."

Psychiatrist says research proves life after death:
". . . Dr. Elisabeth Kubler-Ross, who claims her extensive research on terminally ill and near-dead patients has proved there is life after death, was in Dallas Thursday. She said that some people who exhibit no heartbeat, brainwave, or respiration can tell exactly how many persons came into the room or left the room while they were clinically dead. They can even hear the physician pronouncing them dead. 'Immediately at the transition from life,' she said, 'they all had a sensation of peace and physical wholeness . . .'"

He had always been rather flip when it came to discussing the big questions, but I now believe that it actually went much deeper than he let on. It was not "boring" science that he objected to. It was my rejection of the supernatural.

In the same file, I find a letter to my mother written two weeks before his death:

In answer, Marcy . . .
. . . to your letter requesting that I tell Hal "there is a God before you leave this earth," please be assured that I have done so many times in years past.

I have never denied there is a God, only that I didn't take other people's word for who or what he or she might be. My main denial has been, and continues to be, of organized religion.

71

If Hal, in her mind wishes to believe there is no God, that should be her right, just so long as she doesn't try and force that belief on others. And, she has never tried to convince me there is no God.

I do believe in a God of something, or of someone, a Supreme Being who is out there calling the shots. We all have our own gods, and the world will be a better place when we can refrain from forcing our private gods upon others.

With best regards,
Dave

XIII

TODAY WE WERE seeing the "main" doctor, Doctor Ricard. The examining room was cold (the better to keep the stethoscopes chilly) and bright. Fluorescent bulbs hummed like a refrigerator. Stainless steel light tables were hung on one wall, but no X-rays were on view. Dad hadn't been shown them yet. He wasn't sure he wanted to see the damn thing enthroned on his larynx, like a drunken despot.

I was dressed for the heat, and I sat shivering, hugging myself for warmth. My bare arms and legs were goosebumpy.

"Want my gown?" Dad offered. There was one folded on the examining table. He hadn't needed to change out of his "civvies."

I laughed. Dad thought it would be perfectly all right for me to swaddle up while waiting for the doctor.

"The doctor won't mind. Hell, they don't care what you look like around here as long as you're insured."

Presently, Dr. Ricard came in with Dad's file.

"Doctor!" Dad turned on like a vaudevillian when the curtain is raised. "You haven't had the pleasure of meeting my youngest. Hal, Doctor Ricard. She is older than she looks— and smarter than she sounds, I should add. She's not as old as a baby boomer, but she was born the year of the Big Bang, or actually in the year that they discovered evidence for the Big Bang, to be perfectly precise. The year was 1965 when the universe was discovered to be expanding. She had been added to it. The background noise of the Big Bang, the fading echo, heretofore undetected by scientists, was swelled by her little cry. She made audible that which no man had heard before."

Stochastic resonance, I thought. I looked at him, amazed and flattered.

73

He continued. "But truth is, she didn't cry much. She was a good baby. Kept to herself while her mother looked after bigger problems. Self-sufficient from the start. Opened her own cans of baby formula. Never wailed for things she needed. There were times, though, when she would whimper to herself softly, when no one was around to hear, as far as she knew. When I looked in on her, she would wipe her eyes and pretend nothing was wrong. I wondered what she'd been thinking. When she got older I used to offer her a penny for her thoughts, but she could never bring herself to sell, though she could have made a million off me, as many times as I asked. I'm afraid I still don't know what she thinks, even when she tells me."

"She's probably thinking she wants her father to beat this tumor," said the doctor.

"Suppose?" Dad made a doubtful face.

"I might not be as self-sufficient as you think."

"You're a MacDonald. You are."

"All right. Enough chitchat. Let's look at the patient."

The doctor peered down Dad's throat, then stepped back to have a look at him, cocked his head, looked closer. He reminded me of an interior decorator evaluating a flower arrangement. Throughout the process my dad was made to look so small, hopeful, cooperative, his mother's good son.

"After treatment is over what's next? I mean, how is the tumor? Is it dead yet? When will we know?"

"It's shrinking," said the doctor. "It's shrinking. Really. Really gone down. We're doing real good. Real good. Most of the shrinkage will occur after the treatment. It's swollen right now from the radiation. Then we'll see. You'll have regular check-ups every three weeks and in two years you can celebrate."

"I won't know for two years if I'm cured?" His voice

cracked. "Shucks, by that time I could get run over by a garbage truck."

On the way home, we stopped by the hospital pharmacy for some super high-calorie drink mix. He walked down the corridor with the swagger of one who had just won a bet with someone he disliked.

"You're in good spirits."

"I was thinking that, with all the hush-hush about genetically engineered mouse viruses and Doctor Ricard's optimism, that they mean to keep me alive. The cure must be around the corner. I'll be damned if that isn't what it is."

He pushed open the pharmacy doors like a gangbuster. He bought extra portions. He was going to be around for a while, and he was going to need it. The woman who sold him the stuff didn't question his purchase. Maybe she too was in on it.

Intelligence has gotten the word ahead of all the troops. The war is over. Little battles go on, but the war is over.

I felt it too, I confess. The knowing smile of the lab technician. The doctor's "You're doing real good, real good" was ringing in my ears. Hospitals didn't deal in false hope as far as I knew. Did they?

XIV

IT WAS TIME for me to return to New York. I could be grateful that during our daily dog walks around the park and treks to the hospital, we had sometimes found the chance to talk. Only with me did he ever think out loud. He told others what he thought sometimes, but only after his mind was already made up. His public thoughts on life had boiled down to his rejection of organized religion; a conviction that the best form of government was a benevolent dictatorship (which was rather at logical odds with his position on religion); the opinion that most kids were a nuisance; a proof that a drink or two and/or a bottle of wine with a meal never hurt (which wasn't true for him, not even close).

On our walks, he often repeated stories, but his repertoire was so extensive and funny that I didn't mind anymore than if he were whistling the same tune. We stopped along the way to talk with neighbors. He could have as many as five full-fledged conversations at various points along the circuit. Whenever Candice saw him take his hat and leash the dog, she knew that she would have at least an hour to herself to steal a nap or play the clarinet.

If she cared to look out the window, she might see him, now under the martin house, gesturing to Mr. Packard about the state of the union. Now by the bench, pointing with Charlie's leash at the sickly maple, talking to Mrs. Gerard, whom he simply called "Sweetheart" because he couldn't remember her first name. (He had a lot of "Sweethearts" and "Pals.")

"Hey, Darling," he was saying to his nearest neighbor, "I'd like you to meet my youngest, Halperin. All the way from New York."

"I've heard a lot about you," said the woman. "I'm Dorothy." She was young with short brown hair, wearing a MIT sweatshirt and jeans.

"It's very nice to meet you."

"Dorothy here is a physicist, Hal. The two of you should get together sometime and talk Shakespeare," said Dad.

The woman laughed out loud. "I'd love to," she said. "Have you seen the new *Hamlet?*"

"We watched it together as a matter of fact, just the other night," said Dad. "She explained the whole damn thing. Now I don't understand any of it anymore."

The woman laughed again and continued on her way.

"She would understand your stuff. She's got I don't know how many degrees. You should talk to her, really. Maybe she can give you some advice or something."

"I'd like that."

"Remember the Supercollider that they started to build in Los Collinas? She was working on it."

"They were going to make particles out of potentiality. Re-enact the Big Bang in miniature."

"Oh so you should talk to her. You need to cultivate all the audience you can, since the average redneck is never going to go near your stuff."

I'd been waiting for him to make that argument again. It bothered me that he thought my books weren't worthwhile because they weren't for the masses. Even Shakespeare appealed to the groundlings, he would say with a nod. This time I was ready with an argument.

"Bud gambled that he would get the sheet metal contract for the Supercollider."

"Bud, your mother's redneck friend?"

"When congress scrapped the project, they had to declare bankruptcy because Bud had come to the table with too few dollars. They who have get more. He believed in luck," I went on, "and he counted on a higher power to make events go his particular way."

"He go to your mother's church?"

"No, he was just a superstitious guy who convinced Mom to have faith, first in this investment, later, in lottery tickets. A little philosophy, a little science would have done them both some good, but everyone is so damned scared of boring rednecks, no one tries to teach them."

Dad interrupted me to point out that we had reached the garden.

On that particular turn around the park, we had prepared to gather some herbs from the community garden for me to take home, bringing baggies and clippers.

He had been particularly concerned that we had the right kind of baggies, which had taken some time to locate. Things were done in certain ways, and all you could do was stand aside and try to appear as if you didn't think things might be done otherwise. But never did I feel impatient. I was rather like the acolyte administering to the archbishop. For all the outlandish ritual, the man hadn't gotten to be the archbishop for nothing. And my patience and respect for the ritual gave me a kind of peace.

"Your mother really knows how to pick them."

He cut six or eight sprigs. "You need more? Here, here's more." Another handful cut. "And this is...what is this?" snapping off and rolling it under his nose, "Mint again, but I think it's a wood mint, or a sun mint or..." he sniffed again. "Trouble is your fingers start smelling like mint, and you couldn't tell if it was rosemary."

Parents die when they get old. Where's the tragedy in that? I watched him carefully clip the herbs. Especially if the father in question never took care of his health but has nevertheless somehow managed to drift into the reefy waters of sixty-nine. His death will be the fated one, or, to be more precise, the one selected. He doomed himself with his pipe, bottle, chocolate ice cream, and couch. We are not surprised, but this doesn't make it any easier. Maybe it makes it more difficult, because, I confess, we feel anger at you for having deliberately exposed us to this death of yours. Had you been hit by an errant bus that crashed through the living room window, we couldn't resent you. Now that would be tragedy—in the vulgar sense— because so unlikely. But I feel the real tragedy is the predictable death.

The path is ending. It's almost time for me to get back to New York and start organizing my research notes. Who knows if I will see him again. I want to say good-bye in a special way. One so wants to round everything off, to close the door with a click.

He decided to read the paper for a bit, after which we were going to sit in the garden and talk till my mother arrived to take me to the airport. I sat on the sofa near his armchair reading from a collection of essays on the philosophy of self-organization. He tried to interest me in pages from the paper, an article on a new neutrino finding (which delighted me, since it provided more hope that our universe might continue to expand after all); and a writer who left it all to live in a shack on the Brazos.

Dad had been clipping and mailing articles such as these for years. It was not my habit to read the paper or watch the news, so he took it upon himself to see to it that I at least kept my toe in the river Flux. That afternoon, he peeled an extensive section out and handed it to me with instructions for the circuitous reading route. I started to make my way through "the process of recovering arable land in South Central France." (I had mentioned vague plans about a trip in that direction after Texas, and anything referring to "France" was now perceived as relevant to my interest, as long had been "poetry," "science," and "birds.")

"Ah, look at this," he said. "An article about this guy who's got colon cancer. It says, 'Cancer is not a sentence. It's a word.'"

I wasn't sure what I was expected to say. I hadn't thought the word "cancer" was a grammatical sentence. Perhaps the diagnosis "cancer" was metaphorically a death sentence, but these days people were being cured. Mostly those who had found the tumor in time to remove it. His tumor remained ingrown in his larynx with tentacles driving through the flesh of his entire throat, claiming it like mold in bread.

For Dad the word cancer was ultimately a death sentence as far as I could guess, unless a new treatment was found soon, and no verbal paradox, however true, would save his life. I made a sound that could have indicated either qualified agreement, vague interest, or indignation. But it didn't matter. After he had spoken, Dad heaved a tired sigh and looked blankly at the carpet fringe. After a while his eyes fell closed, he sank a little in his chair, and his breathing deepened to a gentle snore.

I removed his paper, which had started to slide from his lap to the floor, and he gave a ruffled grunt and grabbed a bright advertisement page as if it were a coverlet and gathered it to his chest. After remaining a while swaddled in "Asparagus $1.49 a bundle," he threw away the page and settled more deeply in sleep.

An hour later when my mother arrived, not even Charlie's barking could wake him. I brought my bags to the curb and returned to take another look at him. I didn't want what might be the last goodbye to be all mixed up with the embarrassment of an unintended nap. Final goodbyes are never what you want them to be anyway. I thought, perhaps, I should just let him go on sleeping. There's always that urge to sum it all up, sure and straight, but when you do you leave out all the hesitations and possibilities that seemed very real back when. I took a last look at him sleeping. So what if we failed to decide what to promise or to figure out how to frame goodbye. This is how we honor the love we never proved. Let the last minutes be silent. We both know what we always meant to say.

I was, then, on my way to DFW airport, having been in Texas for almost two months. The crisis had been put down, for the time being. Annie and I did not have to worry that our father was about to jump in front of a garbage truck. Nevertheless, the mental pathways describing his death had been laid, and I could not be satisfied with a remission. Eventually we all die. The question now was whether we might choose to control it or not.

The wipers streaked and smeared greasy dirt on the windshield. The sudden shower vanished and the sun regained itself. Instantly, the streets were dry. The twenty-fourth day of one hundred-plus temperatures. On the horizon, the town of Irving was now a riot of chocolate foam. You could envy them for we were left to squalor in this humid tumescence.

I started thinking about a tiny crime that I had once committed against my father. I must have been eight or so at the time. He had fallen asleep with a big book on his belly. (He'd probably been drinking.) I crept up to him, watching his darting eyes under his fluttering lids, thinking he was playing possum. Armed with a water pistol, I took cover behind the coffee table and aimed at his nose. He woke in an unexpected show of violent anger. I was swept up and spanked thoroughly. In the first seconds, I thought he was just kidding, and I even giggled, which made him even madder.

I finally realized how serious his anger was. It was terrifying to find that events had taken a course I had not intended.

I was extremely sorry. The shock made me pee in my pants a little; I'm still ashamed to confess.

As I drove with my mother to the airport, I decided I needed to tell him that I regretted my mistake, that I knew I hadn't treated him with the respect due a parent. If I did, then he would have an opportunity to apologize to me for his uncontrolled rage at being caught helpless. I remember he had wanted to explain or excuse his behavior that day, but it had just come out, "How could you be so stupid?"

But I should have said good-bye. "Let sleeping giants lie," I sighed aloud. My mother does not mind non sequiturs: everything makes sense to her, given world enough and time. I told her that I was feeling sad that I left without saying goodbye. She wrenched her brows in thought. Later, while we waited for my boarding call, she said with a start, "I know why you missed your last goodbye! So that you will have to come back again before he dies!"

"No Mother. I just made a mistake. I may have to live with that. Not everything works out for the best."

XV

THREE YEARS AGO: We are all in the Cardio Surgery waiting room. When I got the news, I had flown down immediately, despite his insistence that I need not be there for him. "Now, don't come down for this. I don't need it on top of everything else. I know you mean well . . ." But Candice had told me that he secretly wanted me to come, so I did.

I am wondering what I will say to him when he wakes up after surgery: "I'm here, Dad. In Texas. Everything's all right. You didn't die and go to New York. I'm here." He'll get a kick out of that. We can joke about how much he hates New York and how much we are afraid of his dying.

We are all very tired from having risen unusually early. Molly, Annie, and Candice. Old friends of my father's are also here recalling his Mexico City days, men with cinema names, Hiram Wells childhood pal, and "Judge" Sloper former boss, now dear but still imposing, other living caricatures drawn from the Dallas Press Club or Alcoholics Anonymous.

While we silently and separately contemplate the possibility of his death, we wonder, Is Dad a good man or not? Is he loved or is he not? Let's look at his life. Let's look at our shoes and the magazine rack and say nothing.

While waiting I try to read a popular science magazine, an article that said someone has proved mathematically that time has weight. Yes, of course, I think without thinking. Time is change, change is motion, motion is energy, energy is mass, and mass takes up space. That's comforting. Maybe I won't have insomnia anymore. If SpaceTime is material, then I can grab its warm dampish flesh and make it stop haunting me. I'll finally kill that double demon that makes me watch so many anxious nights, hiding in the dark beneath my bed. Ah, but how can time end or begin? How could space be infinitely divided? It makes me sick to think of infinity. But even more horrible is finitude.

At one, an hour past the time that the surgery should have been completed, the doctor enters the room. He is meticulously neat, with polished skin, wearing blue paper cap and smock, blue paperbag slippers. "We had a little trouble," he begins calmly but insensitively, "getting to the fifth artery. It was just too small, but we were able to replace the other four, which should be sufficient after all. We're not to worry about the fifth. He's fine."

Looking down, I notice a drop of my father's bright blood on the doctor's fresh paper slippers.

He continues, "I was surprised that his arteries were that small for such a big man."

Yes, I realize I had always thought of my dad as a big man though he is only five-foot-eight. Suddenly, I am sobbing. The bright blood on sky blue. Judge Sloper is sobbing as well and fleeing the room. We are wretched because now that he is fine, we finally allow ourselves to imagine his not being fine.

Tubes. Digital equipment. Dad is unconscious but uncomfortable, arched back, helpless. His chest is swollen, his neck grotesquely inflamed.

I stand by the side of the cold metal bed, taking his hand. They cracked you open like a nut, Dad. They had your heart out on the stainless steel. Life is no miracle. A body is a thing that can be overhauled and restarted.

"Dad? It's Hali. I'm here."

He can't hear me, can't feel my hand touch his. I have never watched him sleep before. Our attitudes are now reversed. I am watcher and protector. You are the sleeping innocent. How is it that you are still my father, suffering as you do the indignity of that tube shoved down your throat, that machine making you breath with scary regularity?

*   *   *

When he had his open-heart surgery I had stayed in Texas four or five days, reading in his hospital room while he slept. Trouble was, he wouldn't sleep. He felt he had to stay up and chat with me. I could just hear him thinking to himself, *I wish she would go home, so I could get some sleep.*

"That's why being with him through his cancer treatments I was afraid that I might be more of a burden," I said to Seth when I got home from the airport. "I was never sure. I am still not sure."

"He called you know."

"Already?"

"He said you forgot to say goodbye. He remembered something important. He wants you to call him."

"I looked out in the backyard one day—" said Dad, "I remember it was as cold as it gets in Texas. I think we even had some snow. There you were, stacking up an old pile of lumber that you had dragged home from a construction site. You were trying to pull out bent nails with a hammer that was big as your arm. I had promised you that I would help you build an aviary to keep your parakeets in, and I hadn't done it.

"Well, as I sat at my typewriter with four columns to write in two days, I watched you pick up a hacksaw—for metal you know—and proceed to try to cut a two-by-four. I thought, You know Dave, you may have let the other two grow up and get away from you, chasing after boys and such, but you better not lose that one.

"I got my coat, and we went down to the lumber yard and bought plywood, a power saw and a drill."

"I got pretty good with that saw," I said. "We learned how

to frame a window and install a door. Remember we even used some of Grandfather's old tools? The plane. The chisels."

"That's right; we did. You can have them when I go."

"I'd like that."

"Getting the tools, you mean?"

I laughed, glad it was he who made the joke, not I.

"After I'd spent over a thousand dollars on supplies, the store manager finally asked me, How much are those birds worth anyway? I said, My daughter is worth everything to me."

Life doesn't always help you say the things you always meant to say. We were lucky. We were lucky.

"That guy sure thought I was nuts, but I didn't care. Remember when we were finishing the roof? I hammered my thumb like the dickens. I looked down at you and said, Hand me that last shingle. Let's get this done before the pain starts! I hammered that sucker down just in time because the thing had started to throb and turn black as night."

"I remember," I said, I had been amazed at his rare show of self-control.

Before signing off, Dad then mentioned he was now on some list, getting salescalls about some New Age "cures." He was actually jocund about it. He admired their marketing research. Most cancer patients were older, financially secure, and had nothing to lose.

"I admit I was sort of taken in a few years back, but these days I'm not interested in alternative treatments. I'll go with the high tech doctors. I know that's an unpopular line to take. Everybody supposes natural treatments deserve the solemn respect due noble minority groups—unfairly marginalized by the accident of birth—just because no one thought them up in a laboratory. How could Nature have anticipated every stupid thing that man could do to himself and concocted a cure in advance?"

Dad was still convinced the doctors and the molecular biologists were getting close to an all-out cure. Why else would they be wasting treatment on him? There had been recent reports of a genetically re-engineered virus that invaded brain tumors, causing them to become benign. And to think, I mused to myself, the word "virus" comes from the same root as "virile," for life. How aptly named after all! It was an interesting prospect—mankind learning to form a symbiotic relationship with one of our most deadly foes. How lucky! What an unexpected triumph in this 'struggle for life'! Darwin comes along and shifts our attention from generative rules and formal description to the individual scoundrel in the bush, happily digging up truffles.

Together man and virus, in some awesome machine, might someday colonize the entire universe. Leave this sun before it grows cold, find another, and live forever in our young.

XVI

I FOUND MYSELF at a rural train station in arid South France near the Ardèche River (where humankind's earliest representations are to be found on cave walls). The temperature was Texan. The landscape reminded me of Dad's Santa Fe. Premier Klasse from Lyon to Montélimar had not been air-conditioned. My bag contained ten hardcover books. My English landlords arrived late in a funny panel van, with apricots and a fresh baguette for me.

I had taken four rooms with terrace in a cluster of stone towers called "Les Monèdes," which, as Nigel and Mary explained, means, in some archaic dialect, roughly "everything" or "the whole world." We drove up a steep narrow passageway that snaked its way through the "hamlet," as Nigel called it. The hills seemed to have grown these mossy terracotta roofs. The olive orchards and gnarled grapevines and fields of lavender were as old as the forest that lay beyond them. We stopped at a massive rotting wood arch door, with an ancient brass handle, and opened it onto a sun-dappled courtyard of hydrangea and honeysuckle tangles.

I spent my mornings walking along abandoned mine tracks, days gathering feral blackberries to eat or collecting succulents to plant on my terrace wall; evenings reading for my orals and writing poems to send to my father; and nights walking narrow cobblestone streets where bats whirled around lamps. At sunrise, birds flew into the kitchen to eat bread-crumbs on the table while I edited the work from the day before. The scorpions came at dusk.

My bedroom window, framed in ivy, gave upon a view of young Damon who was known in all the fields he has mown. In the village, I was referred to, mistakenly, as the fair, hatted *anglaise,* who smiles politely but says nothing, who came alone for the summer, though some say she has a husband in the States. Some evenings she is heard sobbing as she sits by the light writing.

On Mondays, the open market is held in the square by an austere church whose congregation has all died. I buy fish from a traveling fishmonger. His vehicle is half fish-tank, half truck. He has a desirable frog-body, thin legs, narrow hips, and broad chest. He sells live fish to the villagers, but he kills them for me. I didn't have to ask. He knew.

Returning home, I climb the steep slope with long strides, burdened with fresh *haricots verts,* meaty cantaloupe, and all. Passing Damon—sitting in profile now at *his* window—I return his stare for ten, fifteen, twenty steps, till I am out of view.

I make plans to cook French country food for Seth when I return. I make plans to go to the farmer's market in Union Square. I must be planning to return.

Sometimes I go into the forest in the middle of the night or visit abandoned mines. Sometimes I lie on the church steps and look at the stars. The windows are shuttered on the dead square. A dog barks, twice, four times. Enough. I had never taken the time to see the Milky Way. I see my first shooting star, and a meteor shower as well as rapid, purposeful artificial satellites.

I am growing mint now on my balcony, rosemary, and sage. My father would be happy here. It is a good place to die. You wouldn't feel it. You would just become more of the surroundings, more embedded in your environment than ever before.

After a week had passed I finally phoned Seth from the village. He said he was glad I called. He needed me to write the story about how his father died as an introduction to the catalog for his new collection of paintings. "Do you think you could work on it while you're there?"

"After I finish my book, after my oral exams," I answered. "I'm afraid I'll fuck them up, what with all the other worries on my mind."

"I would like you to write my story as soon as possible for the catalog." As Seth went on to describe the paintings he had in mind, I thought, *My husband has gone insane. It is unlike him to be so dead, so insensitive, so self-absorbed, and now of all times. It must be insanity. I will not have it otherwise.*

I walked to the next village, Banne, and visited their graveyard. Not that I'm morbid. I am not even in awe. I rather think crumbling sepulchers attest more to their own failure than to the fact that a human under a certain name once walked this earth for a precise number of days and was loved. I went there only because the view was excellent and unbelievably dramatic. The graveyard was spread out on top of a windy plateau that towered above miles of flat farms and orchards. The grieving visitors and their dead could observe all with an Olympian perspective.

I plucked a struggling moss rose from a crack in the asphalt walkway and strolled along reading the markers, which the French call "souvenirs." The words *Mon époux* were written on many of them. When I looked the phrase up later, I found it was an archaic term for spouse, now mostly limited to funerary occasions.

It was twilight when I started back. Night would fall by the time I got to the forest. Were there really wild boars about as Nigel had said? I had the option of walking on the road, but I was dressed all in black, and I might look a little foolish. While the light held, I walked quickly, on old medieval pathways, through abandoned terraced orchards and crumbled towers. The scent of feral mint of some long dead peasant filled the air. The forest was old, old, old. Sparse at the bottom, very tall. It had reclaimed farm and garden, but not wholly; some domestic habits had caught on. Nature shared the farmer's rhythm now too. They grew and decayed together.

"Your husband called us looking for you," shouted Nigel from his tower window when I returned to Les Monèdes. I waited till midnight, then I walked down to the square to the phone booth. The connection was instant and perfect. He wanted to tell me that he had bought a pretty Japanese tea set for the two of us to use when I got back. We could sit in the open window on cool nights and watch the Avenue. He got two cups. Only we might drink from them. Come home.

"You know," he said. "You have to convince yourself that there is a good reason to go on. Believe in fate, even though you know intellectually that it makes no sense."

"Okay," I said.

XVII

*WOULD IT BE too arrogant to suppose that we can perturb the
universe enough to keep it open all night? "It is closed," some
say. They cannot believe that luck could do so much. When the
Vatican Council convened upon the hill they asked, "Old light,
tired starlight, climbing out of the last planetary abyss, tell us
what you know. What agency broke the primordial symmetry?
Who gave us these frozen accidents, our laws? But there was
no answer to the question because of the way it was posed.
They failed to understand that a Naked Singularity would not
be like a god at all, except in his absence. He would have no
throne to squat upon, no object in view. He would be but a
symbol, bubbling up in the roiling void. Nothing so grand as
anti-entropic entities like you and I, builders, painters and
celestial mapmakers.*

*So we must believe that if we try to imagine the future for
"Les Monèdes" we will find ourselves humbled, but free. All
behavior is local. I respond to that which is nearest me, and
you respond to me. Try as they might to homogenize the
cosmos, they will never erase what is so particularly here.*

Seth looks like a sleepwalker, when I imagine him being
driven by Franco on his way up Shore Drive to the family
home, arriving six hours later than planned.

Franco, the handy man, had been given the car and the
charge of retrieving Seth from Manhattan at noon, but,
predictably, he had made an unscheduled stop in the Bronx to
show his friends the black BMW sedan. By the time he and
Seth left SoHo it was already close to rush hour and traffic had
been a nightmare.

Seth would have taken the train, had he known. It would
have been quicker and more reliable. Seth had spoken to his

brother once that morning and again briefly in the afternoon. He is there with his father waiting for him. They have just hired a new nurse. The last three were not professional or reliable.

William says that their father refuses to let him feed him. Stubbornness. The only thing he has eaten for days is some lime sherbet and ginger ale.

Only a week before Seth's father had been ambulatory and had gone to see the doctor, who had diagnosed severe dementia. Mr. Cherlin was otherwise physically fit. But for some unexplained reason, he suddenly became bedridden. Now he no longer gets up in the middle of the night to wander through the streets.

The restraints were removed. He lies quietly in bed. He no longer accuses any one of taking things or talking behind his back. Seth says that he has given up and that he wants to go.

Seth's father wears a diaper and has to be spoon-fed, but the twenty-four hour care can be reduced now. Seth's brother has taken charge. They realize that it may be like this for years. The doctor has been encouraging them to consider a nursing home. They can certainly afford it, but Mr. Cherlin would not have wanted that.

A hospital-type bed was installed in the empty room across from the former housekeeper's, now the nurse's, room. Shower doors were removed from the tub so they could lift him in and out more easily. At least, Seth thinks, it is better than the madness; this is only misery. Life will be predictable for many years.

When Franco and Seth finally turn into the long driveway, they see an ambulance. The front door to the house is wide open. Inside the house, the dog is howling. Paramedic radios are heard echoing through the halls. And scattered everywhere is an enormous amount of life-saving equipment. At first Seth can't find his brother. He is in the kitchen weeping and won't let Seth touch him.

Seth goes up the stairs. His father's body lies in bed, as he had died, with the coverlet pulled up and tucked neatly around his chest, a clawlike hand (the one in Seth's painting) clutching the hem. His eyes are open, his expression fierce.

Seth sits in the chair at the foot of the bed and looks at him for a very long time until the coroner finally arrives.

Mr. Cherlin's body was given careful study.It was decided that he probably slipped into a coma and choked on lfuid in his lungs. He apparently had what they were calling "aggressive" Alzheimer's, according to the latest studies in that field. This was a surprise because the doctors had all been certain the week before that he did not have Alzheimer's, but that his dementia had just gotten worse, for whatever reason. But Seth conintued to believe that his father had simply done what he wanted to do, that is to die, by sheer force of will. That was what his father's eyes had said to him.

Three days later, Seth was walking alone on the road. At the time, I lived just a few miles from his mother's in Bridgehampton. I was in my garden barefoot and wearing nothing but a bikini weeding the flowers. He stopped, stared at me dumbly for a long time.

I did my writing. He did his painting. Somewhere in the afternoon we would meet and take the Harley for a ride along the beach, then each return to our separate work. At night he would come back again. I would be sitting on my lighted porch, scribbling away, when I would hear a muffled engine. A single headlamp would inch down the drive. He would enter my tiny cottage. He with olive skin, black curls, I lean and pale, body stuck with Band-Aids masking bugbites and poison ivy. He would steer me into the corner chair.

The first time "I love you" accidentally slipped out, the other said I love you, might have even added "too," then we held each other, feeling sorrow at all the work that lay ahead now. To maintain the fullness of the moment, impossible.

He remembers me in those days always in straw hats and transparent silk—although I believe my wardrobe was less romantic than that. But that is how he thinks of me then and paints me still, like summer ripeness and rain.

No wonder he never acknowledged the past that I had recently run from in New York. I let him think that I was sexually naïve because, who knew? Maybe it was true. Maybe I *was* all innocence and acceptance and freshly-washed skin.

It broke my heart to know that he was only twenty-four, too young to be my lover forever. I had been the girl-mistress to enough married men to have learned firsthand what happened when the seven-year itch started. His reply was that he would never love so well, and so thoroughly and visibly, as when he was twenty-four. He would keep that girl (me) as a token of first love. He was sure it only happened once.

His friends congratulated me for bringing such a change in him. They said he'd been dark and brooding for many years. Was it I or was it the death of his father that had brought the change?

Seth claims his father had to struggle every day to keep himself from becoming more cynical or from doing something corrupt. In so far as I know, he succeeded. In Seth's stories he is only sometimes cruel, never evil.

Seth says he has to make himself into an idealist in order to keep the image of his father at a distance. I think he exaggerates about his father. William remembers a kind man with a strong "life force." I think he *was* a good man, and I think he hated life as Seth thinks he did. I don't know how it realy was the day Mr. Cherlin died, but I don't believe Seth when he says he has dark dreams that he cannot tell. I don't listen when he hints that I am hurt in them.

Seth married me because I don't believe him. I don't believe in evil. I have spent a good deal of my life in seedy places, and still I have never seen evil. It always looks like a misunderstanding of some sort. Pain is never intentional, not really, somehow, and if it is, it could have been prevented, by interceding at the fork.

But if I don't believe in Evil, neither can I believe in Good. Seth, your idealism in marriage, for all its simple beauty, is like a pin balancing on end, theoretically possible, but unlikely in this world. You wanted to make the capture now while your breath was hot and your mind still raced all over my body. And you knew easiness would replace excitement and that too would be fine. Marriage was not the defining goal in your life, the sooner done the better, the better with a girl who understood all this and was relieved to admit it too.

You were brave. I would not have been able to take that step had I been in your position. I would have just let it go. But there wasn't time between your proposal and my answer to think about the impossibilities of marital fidelity. It is insane to promise marriage. You knew it, and so you acted while the madness was still on you. Had we not, we would have missed the one great love. It would have been a courtship broken off violently and with deep regret. You married the girl you loved. I married the man I loved. We would work out the details later. We are doing that now, in our fifth year.

For either of us to live with any other person would be like forcing a bird to live with a beaver. When I first looked at you walking on the road, drowned in thought, I said to myself, "He is my kind."

It's turned out to be true. We can each start at opposite ends of the Met and end up gazing at the same favorite painting. We both love ruts that change course only imperceptibly. Together we found exactly the right shade of carmine for the bedroom, where we sleep protected from the day by lined velvet and deliberate white noise. We follow the body's rhythm rather than the clock's, work at odd hours, and talk in our sleep so that nothing is secret. My words are in your mouth before I can say them. You're not anxious to cure or correct my faults. Nor I yours. (It would ruin our art.) Secrets kept from other spouses are the basis for our understanding. You told me everything that first night, and I told you the worst. And then we went to bed and came clean.

Someone to be unrealistic with, someone to whom to admit self-love. And you understand. And you understand I understand. Whatever you are tempted to do, remember, I've done it, or it's been done to me. I'll be sympathetic. I know why these things happen. Call me to help if you feel the need to stop yourself, my feigning, failing idealist.

XVIII

I STOOD IN the phone booth staring at a dead moth that lay on the shelf. It must have ended its days in a panic, fluttering against the glass while, ironically, the door hung open inches away. It would have been better to have been taken out by a mockingbird. That would have been something. A solid enemy to oppose, not just your own fear of death.

It's better to go healthy and strong, but no one strong and healthy wants to go. One wants to die tired, after a strong healthy day. A sudden stroke would have been better for Dad. Too bad he had his arteries cleaned out or that would have been his way. To think he gave up that death for this one.

But at least his gradual death will not be as much of an affront as a man with a knife at his throat telling him to say his prayers. (Make a note to forbid priest at his bedside.)

I had been in St. Paul Le Jeune for four weeks and had not called Dad. I knew that his treatment would have ended a week or so before. There would have been time for the swelling from the radiation to subside and time for the doctors to run their tests and make their evaluations. Time to come out of French limbo.

His voice was hardly human. It frustrated him that he was "wasting my nickel," unable to speak to me as he wanted.

It was half past one AM in my part of the world. The square was deserted, windows shuttered (but then they were in the daytime too). I stood in the lighted phone booth in the village square standing in odd juxtaposition to the medieval *église* and waited while he put down the phone and gargled with anesthetic. In a moment he was back.

The treatments had been extended up until the week before. He was done now. "The chemo doctor said my recovery was fantastic..." (cupping the phone). "Was that the word he used, Candice?"

"Yes!"

"Fantastic. That's what he said."

Running in Ardèche. Tomorrow I go home. *When I get to the end of my life I will have written nine to fifteen novels, three monographs on narrative theory, one big book of poems, and five screenplays; I will have raised one child, seen him or her have a child. Will I want to stick around after that? Will I even want a soul, ghost, or spirit of mine to survive my bodily death? I have always feared non-existence, but when I have completed all my work, the end might not seem so black. If only I hadn't been raised to believe in an afterlife. Do Jews, like Mr. Cherlin, find it easier to die?*

While waiting for my plane, there was news of one that had just gone down before us. Sixteen minutes passed between the distress call *"panne"* and the impact. Sixteen minutes listening to the terrible groan of a malfunctioning jet engine while the plane dropped thirty thousand feet. Time to imagine the shock and the ironic sorrow of family behind. They imagining you, in your life's last seconds, fumbling with an orange neon life vest, already sad for them and their horrible knowledge, loss, lack of closure, abrupt nothingness of your being. And knowing you will be identified by your running shoe fished out of the harbor. The leather pumps would have been better, more dignified.

A sudden thoughtless explosion would have been more humane. The image of one's death, protracted in time, is all the hell of dying.

Jet lag now in New York. Nodding off at lunch. Unable to sleep at night. Twenty-four hours awake. Lying in bed beside

Seth *Love isn't an arbitrary feeling, but an image of one that has gone before. Habits make miracles automatic. They provide the cohesion for the congregation and the light in the lamp.* Finally, I lose consciousness. I wake sometime deep in the night, needing to go to the bathroom. Although I have opened my eyes, I cannot remember where I have fallen asleep. The amnesia persists beyond the usual minutes. Lying in bed on a soft feather mattress, the air conditioner is humming, making the room virtually arctic. I don't recognize my own home. I realize I am in a cavernous space, and I stare at steel I-beams in the lofted ceiling, arch alcoves along the walls, enormous carved doors far down at the end of the great room. I feel the cold air wafting over the stone floor. I still don't know where I am, though I know the names of the things I am seeing. A light glows in the windows. Daylight or light from the neighbor's studio? I cannot tell. I get up and walk to the bathroom. In the front hall, I see a soft glow again in the windows that give onto the street, and it troubles me that I cannot decide whether it is natural or artificial light. I still do not know where I am, even after I return and lie back down. The warm body next to me I know is my husband. I do not try to remember his name. It is satisfying enough to know that this is a solid strong husband, those are doors and this is stone.

Our bodies sink together toward the center, and I tuck down the feather comforter around us. Comfort like the warm inside of fresh baked bread in winter. This is why one marries. For the warm body that blindly reaches out for you and clings to you when it thinks not. Clings for security and peace.

XIV

"My mom was sleeping very deeply," said Magdalene. Her mother had died, and it had taken me two days to finally get her on the phone. "You could rouse her a little," she went on with her story, which, she said, she finally needed to tell, "but she would fall right back to sleep. I didn't try to wake her. I figured she just needed the rest. But she didn't wake up the next day. The doctor said there was something wrong. He asked, Did she always sleep like that? I said I thought she was just tired.

"She'd had another stroke a few days before. People don't realize that you don't rush them to the hospital for stroke. There's nothing you can do. Keep her comfortable. Help her rest and hope that she comes around again. The doctor came by the house and stayed with her till eleven at night. He's like one of the family. Treated her like a queen. But then we finally had to take her to the hospital because she was dehydrated.

"At the hospital we found that all her vitals had dropped. She was closing down. The doctor told us not to hope for a change. The priest came to give last rites."

"Was she coherent?" I asked.

"No, not then, but later she was able to tell each of us she loved us, all my brothers and sisters. She said goodbye. Then everything dropped again. Her lungs started to fill with fluid. She couldn't really talk. Katherine was with her, and she was pulling at her oxygen mask, trying to take it off. Katherine asked her if she was trying to say that she wanted to go. She asked, *Are you trying to tell me that you're ready to go, Mom?* Mom said yes by squeezing her hand really hard and pinching the oxygen tube to cut off her own air. The doctors took off the oxygen and at two-thirty that night she dropped again, and we all came down, but she made it through the night, and we kept her on morphine, for the excruciating pain."

"The lupus?"

"Everything."

"The cancer too?"

"Everything. She just was in such pain. But she kept whispering her Hail Marys. That was her favorite prayer. Her eyes were fluttering like she was thinking or dreaming. Every once in a while she would raise her eyebrows as if she could see something she liked.

"One of the nurses gave her a bath," Magdalene said in singsong, "and braided her hair. That set the mood for the whole day. She looked so pretty," Magdalene burst out crying, "like she was ready to go somewhere." She recovered a bit and went on. "I put flowers in her hair, and I went to her house and got her angel statues and pictures of the family and put them all over the room so that she could see them.

"Her friend, Beatrice, is real religious. They both liked a famous singer, I forget his name, but he has a beautiful voice and sings religious songs. She and Mom used to pretend that he was their boyfriend, and was singing to them.

"God was in that room. I could feel it. My mom was moving her lips and saying her Hail Marys. She raised her eyebrows now and then.

"At two-thirty again—that was her time—her lungs had filled with fluid again, and her breathing sounded like coffee percolating, and you could smell the sickness of the fluid in her lungs, but at the last her breathing was clear and smooth. The sound stopped, and I couldn't smell the sickness anymore. Jesus was already healing her body for heaven. I believe that.

"I was holding her hand and kissing her face and telling her I loved her.

"Beatrice's tape was playing her favorite song, "Amazing Grace," and everything went according to the tone that the nurse had started when she braided her hair and made her beautiful.

"My mom's sister was there. She had driven from Alabama, and she said to me I should go home because she had come to give us all a break. If not, she might as well go herself. I told her she could stay or go, either way. I would understand, but I was not leaving.

"Then I remembered that one time Mom had said something about wanting to die alone because she knew that it would hurt us all too much to be there when it happened.

"So I said, *Mom I want you to know that if you think it's your time and you're ready, I want you to go.*"

This made me cry, but Magdalene went on.

"*And everyone knows that you love them,* I said, *and we all love you. So I'm going to go outside and pray for a while. And if it's time for you to go, I want you to go.*

"I went downstairs and said Hail Marys for fifteen minutes. Then I went back up. She was still there." Magdalene laughed softly at herself. "I lay down next to her and fell asleep. At two-thirty my aunt woke me, and said, 'She's going.' I took my mom's hand and told her she wouldn't feel pain anymore, and that I wanted her to go, and we all loved her, and we knew she loved us. Her eyes were open, then she closed her eyes, and her heart stopped. My aunt said that she had passed." Magdalene paused, then said, "Hali, I screamed! I screamed!"

This breaks my heart, Magdalene. This I cannot bear. I know why you screamed!

"I can't do anything. I just want to sleep," she went on, sobbing.

"Don't feel like you have to. Stay in bed and cry. I'm sending you groceries for the month."

"Thank you," she said pathetically. "I don't want to iron my clothes for the service or take a bath or do my make-up or anything."

"No, no. Don't pull yourself together if you don't want to. If anyone tells you to, fall apart at their feet."

She laughed, sniffling.

"It will hurt for a long time that you will not see her again."

"I went over to her house and lay in her bed," continued Magdalene. "I just wanted to sleep, not do anything, and be near the smell of her powders and creams. The smell of her hair and skin," she added, voice breaking. "I hate the night at two-thirty. I feel sick."

"You screamed. You screamed, Magdalene. Why did you scream?" I asked, crying myself, hating the answer. She knew, as well as I did, that the dead were dead.

Couldn't ask Dad to go to the funeral for me. He had an MRI today and found another tumor in his right lymph node. Molly's husband Jack called me with the news. Dad could be gone within six or eight months. He said Dad admits now to everybody that he hasn't actually had a reprieve from the pain all this time. Now everything makes sense: the doctor's unconvincing, "Great. You're doing great," all the unpromising facts, my unsturdiness of faith, and my never having begun to hope. There was never any hope, only nothing to lose.

Dear Hal,

This time tumor is growing around his throat and literally choking him. He cannot eat. We are making arrangements with a surgeon to put in a trachea tube and a stomach tube. He will only be in the hospital for a few days, and then we can take him home and feed and care for him ourselves. The plan is to build him up because he is going to need major surgery. Chemo and radiation will not help any more. The only thing to do is to remove the voice box and throat. They will reconstruct the throat afterward. He hasn't yet realized that he doesn't have a choice.

As usual, he has accepted it much better than I. I cannot talk about it at all. Please don't call for a few days. Let me get a better hold on myself. He said he would like to try to call you this weekend. If not, I'll have him email you.

Love,
Candice

Dear Candice:

I have felt, all along, that the treatment was a kind of ritual performed for our benefit. Dad and you have given us months of hope. Thanks for being so strong for us.

I will be there on Wednesday, if I can get a plane ticket. I will stay until Oct 28th (I have to give a lecture on the 29th). Then I will come back to spend as much time with Dad while he still has his voice. My decision to come right away is an instinctual reaction. I cannot do otherwise, so tell him not to wonder whether or not I should or shouldn't come. Will I be of any help to you?

I love you.
H

Dear Hal,

I want you to know that we were going for a cure! There still is a chance left. If you want my honest opinion, I would wait until next week. Your Dad is in the hospital this evening. They are going to operate tomorrow and put in the trachea and stomach tubes. He will only be there four or five days, then he can come home. In order to speak, he will have to cover the trachea tube. It will be difficult but not impossible.

I know how hard this is, but the only hope he has is to have more surgery next month. No more radiation or chemo will shrink the tumor. As I said, it grew one and a half inches in three weeks. He will have a choice of having the surgery or not. He needs to be feeling better, more nourishment, and less pain before he decides what to do. He only weighs a hundred and twenty-five pounds.

I'll let you know tomorrow after this surgery. I feel you need to know the horrible truth. I'm not certain Annie and Molly realize the situation yet. I will call Molly in the morning and tell her so all of you can prepare yourselves.

He will not be calling you this weekend. Maybe when he gets home he will be able to talk some. I'm really hurting, as I'm certain you are.

Love,
Candice

Dear Candice,

As I understand it, the surgery to remove the throat and voice box does not promise much in the way of total recovery. Of course, Dad may surprise us and opt for the surgery. He has really been quite the fighter. He knows we would like him just as much without his voice. He'll no doubt find some way of communicating. He won't be able to eat, but he has had nothing but shakes so long now anyway. What scares me, and must scare him too, is the risk involved in the surgery itself. Molly says he only has a thirty percent chance of surviving it. I don't know if I can face that. I don't know what's worse. It seems like making the choice is the horrible part. Just knowing he has to make it is tearing me apart.

Hi!

Thanks for your support and understanding. You are right, they do not know if he can survive the surgery. But if the tumor has penetrated the lining of the back of the throat, which protects the spinal cord, they cannot even attempt it. I know you want to be here and do what you can. I understand. I'm

not certain when he can come home or what condition he will
be in.

   Love ya,
   Candice

"If he does survive," said Molly on the phone, "he will not be able to speak, and it will not be possible, as was hoped, that his throat could be reconstructed, so he'll never eat normally again. Annie is still plodding along the path of hope. Giving up is not an option. A one percent chance of recovery is enough for her to keep going."

"If there's nothing to lose by hoping, then she's right." My little Pascalian Annie.

When I told Seth the news, he said, "He may hang on for a while. Doctors always say three months, but some patients go for years."

"Yes," I said. "Now that he has had the trachea tube and stomach tubes, he won't starve or suffocate. But maybe the pain will kill him."

"I thought he was on morphine?"

"Still." I paused. Across the loft the phone was ringing.

"Let it go," he said. Now, he was going to talk to me about my father; now he was going to take my hand in such a way that would make me cry like a baby.

"I didn't realize this thing had you so upset," he said.

"I'm afraid of dying. I think my father must be too. It hurts me to think he might be scared."

"It's normal to be afraid of dying."

"My poor Dad, having to agree to surgery when he knows there's a seventy percent chance of dying on the table. Imagine the fear and loneliness that he will feel when he is going under in that cold sterile operating room, a masked face his last image, only indifferent voices around him, no one to hold his hand."

"You know Halibut, maybe you shouldn't think of it that way. Sounds like they are going to do a mercy operation," he said. "When doctors know that someone hasn't got much of a chance of recovery, they go ahead and risk a radical operation, knowing the patient will probably die on the table. It's spares the family."

"You're right, Seth!" Suddenly I saw the whole scene differently. There wasn't a seventy percent chance that he would die but a thirty percent chance that he would survive. "Dad will go under anesthesia believing that he is still fighting for life! That's a whole different picture. It's beautiful," I cried. "You just made everything okay, Seth!"

Seth hugged me. "It's out of your hands, honey."

And no one, not even the doctors, will have to say they are for euthanasia. Good, good doctors. Merciful doctors. The universe is benign after all, I thought.

Dear Hal,

I got your email yesterday, but immediately afterward received a call from his doctor to meet him at the hospital. It was late when I got home, so I decided to wait until this morning.

We know now that all biopsies came back as alive and growing. The tumor is very large and has penetrated the lining behind the throat, making surgery not even an option. He cannot have any more radiation and no chemo will kill it. He has the option to talk to the oncologist about trying to shrink it, but there is no cure. I don't want him enduring any more pain if it can't be cured. However, it is his decision. He will come home Wednesday, and the doc thought we had about six months. He is on heavy pain medicine, but seems alert and comfortable.

You can stay here if you like. We want to make the most of the time. Perhaps you can do some things and have lots of good talk time. We need to use this time when he feels like company.

He will be at his best the first few months, and that would be the best time to be here. Once he reaches the unconscious stage, it will not be as important. We will keep him at home as long as we can, I don't want him in the hospital until the end. I love you. I'm hurting like hell.

Candice

Annie's voice was tiny, as if she were only three or four. She was keeping her voice down because Dad was sleeping and she was calling from his bedside phone. "I just fed him. He's resting now. He's had his morphine, but he's feeling pretty bad."

"Can he eat?"

"A little shake. He's got a feeding tube." She spoke in that same singsong Magdalene had used.

I haven't called Texas now for three days. On that end I doubt anyone notices. Each will assume that I am in touch with the other. But I am avoiding them and their knowledge. Trying to put it at a distance. Why? So that I may concentrate on my studies? No, I haven't read a book in days. What have I been doing? Working on Seth's story about his father. And every day I run ten miles along the Hudson River, even if it rains.

Meanwhile, my family probably supposes I am as deeply invested in the stringy matter of the thing. Well, I'm not. I'm running. Running. Just a little more time, please.

XX

I ARRIVE IN Texas for another short visit, before the inevitable long one. He looks like a little boy again, head grown larger, like all old, very old people. (He is not that old.) His teeth seem larger because his lips have grown thinner. But he is up, dressed now. The tube in his throat gurgles. His eyes are big and round like Annie's. His skin has a nice sheen. Annie has cut his hair, and he looks tidy and trim, a little like Tony Randall. He reads his paper, walks the dog, swishes coffee around in his mouth, and then spits it out. He watches TV and slips away every three hours or so.

He wants me to see how his morphine is administered through his stomach tube. He lies in bed, dressed in shorts and a button-down shirt. He pulls up his shirt to free the tube. He and Candice unstopper it. She shows me how to measure and mix the dose. He keeps the tube pinched to keep his lunch (a sky-blue vanilla liquid) from backing up. She inserts the head of a large syringe into the tube and injects the morphine. Then she puts a funnel in the end of the tube and pours water in to flush the medicine down.

"I used to be fascinated by the body," he says, covering his trachea tube. "But now my heart's been replumbed. My throat's been sealed shut, and I get watered by a garden hose. Pretty low-tech."

Candice and Dad are angry that one of the doctors suggested more chemo and radiation. It's one of the fastest growing tumors they've seen, and they said they wanted him for research. Candice knows that would be a good thing to do, but he's had enough. He's had enough, she says, crying.

She is trapped in angry helplessness. She is a good woman and good women always find a way to improve things. But

110

what can she do here? Right now she is planting a hundred pansies outside the window where Dad can see them because he loves their pensive faces. His mother died with a pot of pansies watching her, I have often heard him say.

He said that he had planned to plant hyacinth bulbs himself because he likes the way they pop up in the early spring before the first mowing. "Ah, but what the hell for?" he says, sighing.

"You could plant them for Candice. Every spring to be reminded. A delayed gift."

He notices Candice walking by the open bedroom door, and he remembers that his Kleenex box is empty and tries to call to her. No voice comes out. His hand flies to his trachea tube, fumbles with the opening, and finally he is able to say her name, but by this time she is already too far away to hear.

"Why don't we get you a bell or an air horn like Harpo Marx?"

"Candice will feel like stuffing it up my nose," he pauses to breathe, "at the end of two weeks."

"Snap your fingers then."

"Oh, that'll be real nice for her."

"She won't mind, and you know it. It would hurt her to know there was something you wanted and didn't ask her for it. I know. Why don't you put a music box on the nightstand and open the lid when you want something? A music box tinkling away won't sound demanding at all."

"You'll come back here, one afternoon, following the sound of the music box. And I'll be gone. You'll never know what I wanted to say. You can suppose," he took a breath, "the meaning of the universe had finally been revealed to me. And I wanted to tell you about it. Or. I was going to divulge where I stashed a trunk of sterling silver. Your inheritance."

"I will probably just suppose you were thirsty."

"Music boxes don't run long. If you miss my last request, you'll probably never know it."

"Yes we will. The lid will be left open and everything still inside."

"I ever tell you about the time," he paused to breathe, "my dad took me to the old homestead in Kilmarnock? Handed me a lump of coal. From off the ground." He shows me the invisible lump. "Said, 'Here, son. Here is your inheritance. What's left of it.'" He takes a moment to breathe, then continues, "Lost a million dollars. That was a lot of money back then. Greed. They dug too deep. Flooded the mine. I'm sorry I don't have money to leave you either."

"I won't ever need it."

"I should have had. Some financial advice. From that husband of yours. Too late."

"I'll take Uncle Halperin's pewter brush set."

"I think I promised that. To Fizzlebritches. Oh, you two fight it out between yourselves."

"Dad, I'll see you tomorrow. I just stopped in for a quick hello. I don't want to tire you."

"Okay. When are you coming back?"

"Annie and I are going to pick up Molly at her office. We were thinking we might get a bite to eat together."

"So you won't be back till tonight?"

"I'm staying with Mother again."

"Oh yeah, okay. You should spend time. With your mother. Don't forget your mother."

He seems like a desperate little boy, but I leave him because he needs sleep, and I don't want to talk to him about his death, not yet.

The last seating on an Indian summer night, back porch of a BBQ restaurant. We order green salads and ice tea in barrel-size cups. Annie is steeped in regret that a cure somehow couldn't be found. Molly is doing what he would want her to do, taking care of her life and the business Dad has left her. I am thinking too much.

I am trying not to think about Seth's dead stare when I change the subject from his father to my father. I cherish the one or two kind words that he has made. The problems will go away once the whole thing is over. Then our relationship will go back to normal, working side by side, sharing meals, walks, and talks about his paintings.

My sisters and I will each have our own special version of the nightmare, but just now, the weather is superb. The night couldn't be more lovely. There is no one, not even Seth, who knows me right now, knows my fears, better than my sisters do.

The air is balmy, and there are still a few crickets hemmed around in the dark, and I imagine I will look back on this as the Edenic eye of the storm. We blame our mother for making us hate our father. We each wonder what the next six months will be like, but it's too soon to wonder out loud. He'll slip into a coma, then he will go to the hospital where we hope they will not feed him anymore through his tube.

"He likes his morphine. It doesn't cloud his thinking or make him depressed. The doctor says to give him as much as he wants," says Annie.

"The tumor is as big as a fist."

"It seems as important for us to spend time together tonight, since Dad is going," I say, "and we will be left. It's our pain, this death of his."

"I hope that when I am dying I will be able to say 'This is a good time to die,'" says Molly.

"Not me," I say.

Molly laughs.

"I want to be old, gaseous, with but a few wispy white strands stuck to my scalp, my head lopped forward on my chest, like a dead rosebud, unable to recognize my family, having lost all sense of such concepts as life, death, or feeling."

"I want to be shot by Clint Eastwood in a black hat. I'm running, wearing a torn dress. Clint is shouting, 'I told you you could never leave me.'"

"You married a Clint Eastwood, didn't you?"

Molly sighs. "I guess I did." After a while she adds, "He's been great through this whole thing. Really trying to help. I've been awful."

"Seth and I don't talk about it much."

"Well Hal, you are a strong woman. He knows that."

Strong as a piece of crystal with a fault running right down the center. Laughing I say, "He chose this time to become interested in some girl called April. It's good for his art, he says."

"You're too honest with each other. You should keep up appearances," says Annie.

"But who can he talk to if not to me? The problem is I *do* understand. I think he's making a mistake, but I understand why."

"You should tell Seth that you're upset about Dad and that you need extra sympathy," says Molly.

"Oh I get it from you two and Magdalene. Besides, that's not something I can ask for. And anyway, there's something else. It's not simply that he's being insensitive. There's something about his father's death that I don't understand."

"Hi Dad," I peek in on him before going on to Mother's. I don't want to stay long. "You get enough to eat? You want your medicine?"

He covers his trachea tube to speak. "Where's Candice?"

"She's in the kitchen with Annie and Molly."

"We haven't got much time." He grabs my hand. "Now listen. I don't want to set a bad example."

His words are rushed. He's going to ask. He's just blurting it out.

"This isn't the way out of your problems. Generally speaking."

"I'm coming right back Dad," I say, interrupting.

I have come here before in my thoughts, half convinced that I have been perverse for doing so. It is like stepping into the shadow that has long been cast before me. "Seth and I both will be here for Thanksgiving."

He starts to try to talk again, but can't get enough air. His eyes are especially big and clear blue and wander all over the room. Between every few words, he pauses to breathe. "I was a little worried—asking you about this—because you've tried that kind of thing before. I'm talking about suicide. How do you feel about it? I mean, you don't think about it anymore, do you?"

Blood rushes to my head, and I can feel my pulse beating in my ears. I hear myself say, "I haven't tried it again since I stopped believing in God."

"Well, that was the other thing. I know you don't have religious thoughts to hold you back. We don't have much time."

"I said I'm coming right back."

"Well, I don't know how I'll be."

"If anything happens, Candice will call, and I'll come immediately. Eight hours at the most." I take his hand, something I have never done before. "Dad, I knew you would ask me." As I speak, I watch myself from the telescoped distance of the last five months. This is what anticipation does to you. It takes you out of the present. "I've been thinking about nothing else all summer. I'll do anything you ask. I don't want to, but I'll do it."

He smiles sadly.

"Did Annie ever tell you about her dream?"

"No," he says, full of concern.

"She dreamt you two were in our old motorboat in Cedar Creek Lake. You drop a flashlight in the murky green water, and you say, You know what I'm going to do, and I don't want you to try to stop me. Then you jump overboard. She doesn't know what to do, respect your wishes or stop you. It was awful. It really upset her."

Dad listens with open mouth; his eyes fill with tears. "Oh poor Fizzlebritches. I didn't know that. She didn't tell me."

"It's so hard to know what you really want."

"I don't want to die crapping all over myself."

"I promise I won't let anyone keep your body alive without you. I promise."

"I saw an article. In the paper. Said how putting your sick dog down is the humane thing to do. Now why can't they do that for people? I bought some ammo."

How does my face look to him as I absorb these words? is all I can think. Then suddenly the past catches up to the present. I am fully in it with Dad. I let go and start sobbing.

He is surprised! He looks at me, startled, surprised that I should cry about my father wanting to blow his head off.

"No, Daddy, please don't. Candice. No, don't. We can't find you like that. There's a better way. We'll just stop feeding you or give you too much morphine."

"It takes eight to twelve days to starve."

"Maybe not so many."

"I might not have enough morphine."

"Don't do this to spare us pain."

"I'm being totally selfish."

"You are never selfish."

"This time."

"You know you may feel like you want to do it now, but you may not want to when it comes down to it. We can wait for it to happen on its own. Oh don't you wish you could slip in the foyer and hit your head?"

"If you can arrange that I would prefer it."

"I'll get you whatever drugs you want."

"Maybe the car. Run a plastic tube from the muffler. Candice could be out shopping."

"She cannot find you there like that. That's not the way. How am I going to sit beside you if you do it like that? There's no need to do it like that. You can die of dehydration in three days."

"Some claim that's painful."

"We'll just give you an overdose."

"You tried it. Didn't you take enough? We can't do that. It might not work."

"They pumped my stomach. Nobody will do that to you."

"I want to be sure."

"Can't we just call the doctor, ask him to prescribe something?"

"Not my doctor. This is Texas. We can't tell anyone. Do you understand? Suicide is illegal. There is a book published by the Hemlock Society. Tells you how to do it. With leftovers from the medicine cabinet. Mix with alcohol. I wanted to send away for it but was afraid Candice would see it."

"I'll get it."

"It even tells you about the plastic bag method. Put it over my head."

"Oh no Dad, I couldn't do that. It won't be necessary."

"It's supposed to be effective."

"I'll get the book. We'll do it right. Don't worry. We're not going to put you in a diaper or anything like that. I thought we could just let you slip into unconsciousness."

"What's the point of waiting?"

"Don't think your death is going to bring us relief. It won't. That's when the real pain will start."

"I did it for my father."

XXI

I GOT TO my mother's house and pulled my bag inside. I discovered I was displacing my mother's "friend," a mooch she met through her church, whose articles of clothing and personal junk littered my former room. "Hi," I said tiredly. Nelson said nothing. He silently watched me heave my heavy bag onto the bed, then went off to find my mother. I moved a pile of clothes from the seat of the chair to the floor and sat heavily at the writing desk.

Think about why you would do what you would. You like to control situations. Stop certain things from happening. For example, you would like to prevent Annie's nightmare from becoming a fact. That's all. You won't let him take his own life. You would rather do it for him, painful as it would be.

But don't do what you may regret when you are of a different mind. You think you know what you're doing now, that you're of sound mind and body, but the world will have a different meaning tomorrow. And right and wrong will be slightly shifted. You think you know what you are doing. You think you have volition. A complex knee-jerk may be all anyone's willed acts amount to.

Imagine jumpers. They must regret it immediately after the twitch. People who try to overdose can call an ambulance or drag themselves into a busy hall. Using a gun lets you avoid facing the awful fact that you've just taken your own life— unless the first shot doesn't kill you right away. I've heard of that happening. The skull is as thick as a stone cottage, and the brain is not vital in every spot. It could happen.

"She just threw my things on the floor. Now they're wrinkled," said Nelson.

I turned and saw Nelson and my mother standing in the doorway.

"Nelson," I said, jumping up. "Why don't you try to imagine that I might have more on my mind than whether or not your polyester crap gets more wrinkled than it already is. Don't push me. I'm not stable. If you don't shut up—"

"You're fucking crazy," Nelson screamed back, then began to return his clothes to the chair.

"Hal honey, you're just upset about your father because of your shallow disbelief in God. Look to God."

"My disbelief runs to the core."

"How could you say that to her?" demanded Nelson. "That's why no one in your family really likes you. You're a snob, always trying to sound so smart."

That hurt. I knew Nelson must have gotten that information from somewhere. "I'm not trying to sound smart. I just think out loud too much. If I wanted to sound smart to you, Nelson, I would just repeat your own clichés."

"You need to ask God to help you."

"Why have you come here anyway?" my mother pleaded. "I don't know why you don't stay with your father," she added helplessly.

"He and Candice might want to be alone," I said doubtfully. "I thought you might want me to stay here. Don't kick me out again, Mother, because someone tells you it's what God wants."

"I *do* want you to stay," she said, starting to cry.

"I'm sorry Mom."

"Well I don't want you to stay," said Nelson.

"Nelson, can't you show a little Christian sympathy?"

"It's God's will that he should die," he said.

"You don't understand," I said finally.

"Everybody in the family is going through the same thing," said my mother.

"No, they are not. I cannot tell you why, but trust me. Give me sympathy. Pretend you think I'm weak. Maybe that will help. Feel sorry for me, just tonight. Just for an hour till I can get to sleep."

"You think you're so damned special. You need to look at yourself in the mirror. You need to . . ." Nelson kept talking till I wanted to put my hand over his mouth. I stopped hearing him and watched his thin lips moving. I went toward him, reaching out my hand to his face. When I got close, Nelson grew frightened and kicked me. My m`other screamed.

"How can he ask you that?" asked Seth over the phone.

"It's ritual. Some kind of ceremony, that's why. He wants to act his death. He wants to control it, and he wants me to participate."

"I don't want a court . . ."

"Don't talk like that!" I spoke through my tears like a cripple who manages to run. "I know it's illegal, but that is in the outside world. Those things don't count here."

"You're not making sense. You're in the Bible Belt. The jury would have no sympathy for you. Be logical."

"There are other kinds of logic," I cried. "It's a ritual. Why else would he ask me? He's had time and opportunity to write the Hemlock Society on his own, get the drugs. Why didn't he? Because he doesn't want to die alone. It's something he needs to do with me, with my help."

"How can he ask you to do that? I'm mad at him for asking. It's perverse. You shouldn't have to take on the responsibility."

"You have no right. You just don't understand."

"My father asked me. I said no." It went quiet on Seth's end.

I waited a while and said, "This is different. My father's sick. He never wanted to be a burden."

"You expected this?"

"All my life. But especially this summer. But it was weird the *way* he asked. He was so impatient about it. So hasty. The morphine must make him less emotional, and it's hard for him to talk. He hasn't got the breath to beat around the bush."

"Oh I feel so bad for you, Halibut."

"My mother and Nelson tell me I just need to pray. Nelson just wouldn't shut up. I lost my head. All I could think about was covering his mouth. It just kept moving," I laughed. "But then he got scared or mad and kicked me."

"Did he hurt you?" asked Seth angrily, ready to defend me.

"It's my mother that hurts me."

"Your mother and Nelson are nuts. I don't want you to be there. Come back to New York where you don't have all those crazy religious people to deal with."

I started to sob harder. "It means a lot to me that you understand how awful it is here. But I knew it would be. I've known all along he would ask me. It was my first thought after I found out he had cancer. I've been wondering all this time if I were sick or something for being so morbid. Do you see now what was bothering me all summer?"

"I feel so sorry for you," he whispered. "And I've been going on to you about April and my own father. That's so sad, it's almost comical. I thought you were just concerned about your oral exams. You're always excluding me when you go run off to read. I wish I could hug you. Halibut, tender Halibut."

"Thanks, Seth," I said recovering, "I'm probably better off here in Texas. I need to be with my sisters and Candice. With them it's okay to cry or to joke, or to just go on doing normal everyday things, whatever. They won't judge me or feel burdened. I don't have to expect them to treat me special. Do you know what I mean? Because I know they know. I think I should move to Dad and Candice's tonight. I hope I won't be putting them out."

"I don't know why you always worry about that."

I called Candice, and she said, 'Come. Stay here, honey. We didn't want to take you away from your mom, but you know your dad likes having you around.'

I didn't know, not really, not for sure. And it was good to hear Candice say it.

Today I told my dad that I didn't want him to be misled by our being able to keep our spirits up around him. I assured him that we bawled our eyes out the minute his back was turned. Then I asked him if he had cried yet, about dying. "Crying is good for you," I said. "Relieves stress, calms you down."

He said he didn't cry much, except during movies. "When someone does something mean to someone else." And he said he had cried watching *The English Patient* when the woman died.

"Yeah," I said. "I did too. I cried for the survivor. Think of us without you and cry. Because we will miss you, and it's going to be just plain sad." My eyes watered, and he smiled at me and squeezed my hand.

He began to close his eyes. The afternoon dose of morphine I had administered was beginning to take effect. But suddenly his eyes sprang open again. "Did you order that book?"

"It was easy to find. It's a bestseller."

"People are dying to read it."

"That's so obvious, it's funny. I didn't read it carefully yet, but glancing through, I gathered it does not advise taking drastic measures. People are more willing or able to let family die than you might think. It says that ninety-five percent of all intensive care nurses have assisted the death of terminally ill patients. No one needs to talk about it. It's quietly done. When you slip into unconsciousness, we will stop giving you food and water, stop vacuuming your lungs, and we'll up the morphine dosage. Magdalene told me that the hospital gave the family the right to order as much morphine as they wanted. Her mother died after three days."

"I don't want to go three days. Stay away from my butt. I don't want anybody cleaning up after me."

"We will get a twenty-four hour nurse for that."

The next day we sorted out his manuscripts, and I went out to make copies of the final drafts for Candice. The originals I would take back to New York. Molly and Annie got various drafts. "They'll have a better chance of surviving if there are many copies in several different places. You always hear of precious manuscripts turning up in unlikely attics a hundred years after the author is dead. And I will do what I can to see them published. I promise."

"I never did much with them."

"You know I won't give up. Eventually, they will be read." I put Candice's copies in neat boxes, labeled, and stacked them on his office shelf. *We're putting your effects in order, Dad.* "You don't have that many rejection letters. You didn't try hard enough," I said. "Every great novel needs at least a dozen before it gets accepted."

He shrugged his shoulders. "I gave it a shot. Mr. Maddox didn't want it."

Mr. Maddox's criticism: "too literary," "not dramatic enough," "episodic," but the real blow was the observation that "the hero is not particularly likeable" because the hero was really Dave MacDonald himself.

"In other words," I said, "it's not a dime-store novel."

He shrugged again, then put his hand over his trachea and inhaled deeply. "I wrote it the way I wrote it because that's the way it was."

"I'll have his letter quoted on the back cover when it finally does come out."

He smiled. Then, though he really was too weak to be out, he asked me to take him on an errand.

As his daughter, I couldn't argue. He had the idea that he needed a special kind of amber bottle in which to stash morphine. He planned to order extra every week over the next few months, and he hoped Candice wouldn't notice.

"She hates drugs," he said. "I read that amber keeps the drugs potent. We'll need to get a couple, then we'll find a hiding place."

I didn't argue or question his logic. This was ritual.

When we got to Addison he told me to turn into a parking lot near a strip mall. I let him lead us into a Hold Everything store, where we had to crane our necks to look for the thing we wanted in the high shelves. We could only find a cobalt blue dropper bottle, but I convinced him we should go ahead and take it. He insisted he pay. We walked to the checkout counter. His trachea tube, like a plastic cravat, was visible through his open collar. The clerk, though kind and gentle, couldn't keep from staring.

Now we had to drive to a medical supply store, which was much further away but was sure to have what he wanted. Again he insisted upon coming in with me. He looked a little less out-of-place there. His trachea tube looked like the merchandise, he joked. His insisted on asking for the item himself, then dug through his pockets for the couple of bucks. The clerk handed him his purchase in a brown paper bag. Dad emptied the bag and crumpled it along with the receipt, asking the clerk to get rid of it for him. He put the bottle in his pocket.

He could have sent me on the errand alone. He had to be the one. I was just there to take part.

It was now a few days before Halloween. Dad had overtired himself and slept while Snaggle Tooth, Fizzlebritches, and Snakes-in-Hair carved the MacDonald memorial pumpkin without him. I sneaked in to see him before I left for the airport. I only had enough time to tell where I had hidden the suicide manual in his bookshelf.

The book was pretty clear about how difficult it was to kill oneself. One had to take massive amounts to be certain. Most people survive suicide attempts. Dad and I had decided to mix morphine, alcohol, and various other painkillers he had around the house, as described by the book. Seconol was recommended above all else, and it would be my job to find some.

The book recommended the plastic bag in addition, he reminded me.

"I don't want my last image of you to be like that, Dad. Please. Seth's last awful memories of his father are more vivid and tend to replace the good ones that came before. I don't want it to be like that for me."

I told him I would be back in as soon as two weeks. Seth and I planned to come down for Thanksgiving. I supposed he would be feeling better by then. You could say that his health had actually improved in the week since the trachea and stomach tubes had been installed.

A little less than three weeks later I got a call from Dad. Did I have his manuscripts sorted out? His voice was weird, hardly human.

"Yes, Dad. You know I do. We did it together when I was there, remember?"

"Okay. That's all I wanted to know."

"Dad, I wasn't going to come till the end of the week, but now I'm going to get on a plane tomorrow, Okay?"

"Okay. Whatever you want to do."

I heard the receiver being clumsily replaced. I called the airline and booked myself on a flight leaving for Dallas the next day.

XXII

ANNIE WAITED UNTIL we had found the car in the airport garage and stowed my bags before she told me that Dad was in a coma. They found him at seven this morning in front of the television set. He must have gotten up in the middle of the night. Candice's son Greg had come over to move him to his bed.

That's it, then. "But he did know that I was on my way?"

"Yes, Candice told him last night that you were on your way."

He doesn't need my help now, then. Or is now the time for me to help?

Annie said that he had told Greg months before that if anything happened to him, he should look in the file marked "Cancer."

The suicide note? I wondered.

"He wrote his own obituary," Annie explained, crying a little, then she laughed. "It's actually funny. He calls it his 'auto-obit,' and he starts out, 'The pipe finally nailed me, but I enjoyed every aromatic puff.' At the end, he invites everyone to his wake. He says, 'Help me exit laughing.' He also left instructions to sell his car and a receipt for his own cremation that he arranged five years ago. He got a ten-dollar cardboard box for the ashes. He specifically says that's all he wants."

I smiled. That's our dad. We drove out of the airport. After a while I asked, "Any note for me?"

Nothing for me. My importance seems to be diminishing.

Annie also explained that he had indicated in his instructions that he was not to be fed. Candice had been convinced to let him die at home. *They were cooperating,* I thought. *It isn't all on me anymore. We would all, as a family, quicken his death.*

I found Dad lying in his bed, no thinner than he had been weeks before. "I'll leave you two alone," said Candice, and she closed the door.

His face twitched when I stroked it. He seemed more in a deep sleep than a coma. "I'm here Dad. It's me," I said crying. "Here I am. I came like I said I would. I promised. I'm a little late, but I'm here. I'll keep my promise." I sat down next to him and held his hand; he didn't squeeze back, but it still had some life in it.

I am honored, Dad, that you chose me to be your secret accomplice, that you trust me, that you believe I am that strong. But you're leaving me, and I will be left with the others. Maybe I should act for them, if I act, not you.

"You're not going to feel any pain. We'll give you plenty of morphine. Nobody's going to feed you. A nurse is coming to keep you clean and make sure you're comfortable. Candice says we are entitled to free twenty-four hour hospice care." I kissed his fingers. "You're not going to the hospital. Candice won't let them take you."

The house became a waiting room. Life stalled. We sat around repeating what had happened over the past few months, looking for a chance that we might have handled it better, perhaps. What would be my next move? I wondered. Maybe nothing. Maybe find the morphine he stashed and give it to him after everyone had come one last time to say goodbye. I watched the affairs with a solicitousness I vaguely sensed but couldn't own as mine. I felt estranged from my sisters and from Candice because I had a secret.

The day nurse had not shown. We were all hoping that the night nurse would come soon and bring a catheter. This was the most important thing on our minds, keeping him comfortable.

Finally, at six, a night nurse came, but he did not have the equipment we needed. Annie was furious. "Incompetence!" she said as she came into the kitchen from the bedroom to update the rest of us.

I headed toward the bedroom to make sure that the nurse wasn't going to try to put a diaper on him. He was a big man in scrubs with close-cropped blonde hair and a ginger goatee. He explained that the catheter should have been ordered by the agency. Nurses didn't supply that kind of equipment. He said he would put the order in. He was busy cleaning out Dad's congested lungs. Dad winced several times, and I stood by nervously, saying every now and again, "careful," or "not so hard."

The nurse turned and glared at me. "I know what I'm doing. Trust me."

His name was Thomas, but I should call him "Tommy," he said with a strong East Texas accent. He cleaned the equipment and shook out the syringe rather violently, glaring at me again. He would have to make a few phone calls, and he asked us to be patient. Annie looked like she still wanted to kill him. It was not his fault, I could see that, but we didn't know the rules; we only wanted Dad to be comfortable.

Tension eased a little. Annie apologized. Candice went to make food. Then, while we waited for the delivery from the pharmacy, Thomas tried to engage us in small talk. Annie answered his questions, who was who, who lived where, who was the oldest sister, etc. I sat looking at Dad, wondering if he could hear all the chatter around his bedside, and believing that if he could, he would not like the banal informality of it all. Shouldn't we be thinking and talking only about the end of an important human being? Apparently, the nurse had grown immune to such situations and didn't think small talk inappropriate. He chattered on. Then he offered to explain the difference between spiritualism and religion. I could see his garrulousness was caused by his nervous energy over having the luck of finding himself in a household of pretty women, but I was not going to allow him to continue with his assumption that everyone believes in some kind of God, not here, not now.

I finally spoke. "One is superstition, the other institutionalized superstition? At least organized religion makes an effort to come to a consensus that works. Better than valorizing the whims of every freelance nut-case."

Thomas stared dumbly. It was going to be a long night.

At around eleven Candice went to bed in the guestroom. "I can't sleep with a male nurse watching me," she whispered to me in private. We decided I would take the night shift since I was used to staying up till two or three anyway. I was determined to spend most of the night reading beside Dad. He would want that. At five AM or so, I would go to sleep in his office on the floor. That would leave Dad alone with the nurse for only a few hours.

Thomas sat at the foot of the bed facing his patient—and me. I thought perhaps I could ask him to sit down the hall in the TV room. I would call when he was needed. No, I thought, he's going to be quiet. I propped up some pillows and sat on the edge of the bed next to him with my book. I adjusted the reading lamp, leaving Dad in shadow. I opened *Neuronal Man* to the dog-eared page and tried to think about chemical messages, thresholds, and bursting clocks. How random were our thinking processes, I wanted to know. I wanted to believe. I felt the nurse watching me as I read. The room was quiet. The house was silent. The human brain is a very complex organic computer, but a computer that can make mistakes, that's the key. A computer that's a little vague, a little off, a little imperfect, just enough for creativity. Just enough to make one human.

It is my fortune that my memory is melodiously imperfect.
I misremember. I gather strays, oddballs, and even a few of the
enemy along with the loyal under the same heading. Ideas
cohere around the center, while about the edges they flow.
  Without mistakes and misdirection, I would be as dumb as
a cat's beetle, not intending escape, only reacting to claws.
The creative and the insane are more human and alive than
others, this I firmly believe. No, I take it back. The insane have
flown too far, their intelligence dissolved in water. Somewhere
between insect and insane, then.

I glanced at Dad's proud profile and stroked his hair, something I would never dare do to him awake. The nurse recrossed his legs and coughed. I turned a page.

"You're not like your sisters," he said, rather loudly for the hour.

I looked at him for a moment, then looked back at my book.

He went on, "You're holding a lot inside. I can see that." He was glaring at me again. It seemed he couldn't look without glaring. His eyes were deep-set, and his thick lips were pressed tight. "You know if you don't have an outlet, it's going to come back on you."

"Interesting diagnosis," I said in a very low tone, looking at him archly. "Do you think he can hear?" I hinted and went  back to my book.

"Is that for school?"

"In a way."

"What's your major?"

"Teleology," I answered to shut him up.

I could have left the room myself, I suppose, but I didn't want Dad to find himself alone with a stranger. I looked at Dad whose breathing was becoming strained.

"If you would let me do my job, he wouldn't be breathing like that."

"We don't want to put him through unnecessary pain to prolong his life," I said coldly.

"Oh he's going to be around for awhile. A coma can go six months. He's not even in a deep one. As a matter of fact, I think he's got some pain. I'm going to give him another dose."

I watched Thomas measure out the morphine. He also picked up several bottles that were on the nightstand, reading the labels.

"He's been sick a while, hasn't he? You could open a pharmacy with this stuff. Dilaudid. Demerol. Yep."

"Are any of those drugs barbiturates? Isn't it dangerous to mix barbiturates with morphine?"

"*You* don't want to mix anything, girl." Thomas then mentioned that Dad's used morphine patches could get you ten to twenty on the street. "They're a hot item."

I wondered why he thought I might want that kind of information. "I guess if you really need ten or twenty that's something to know."

"You don't look like someone who needs it, money that is. I bet you have a nice life in New York."

"I like my life."

"I can tell. And you like yourself a lot too. Hey, but that's okay. You've got style. I could see that right away, just by your clothes and the food that you eat."

"Lentils?"

"Whatever you call it. That fancy gourmet stuff."

"Dried lentils are sixty-nine cents a pound."

"Stop being so defensive. I'm not criticizing. I think it's cool."

I hoped Dad couldn't hear all this.

I finally gave up the idea of reading and listened to Thomas, who wanted to talk so bad it was comical. I couldn't concentrate anyway. While he spoke with a boyish lisp, he presented me with what he knew to be the best angles of his intense face. Vulgar charm was the one thing he had, and he used it. He told me about his childhood, a mother who betrayed him, and a stepfather who beat him. Reform school. Running away to California at fifteen. Being propositioned on the beach by older couples.

Surprisingly, his grammar wasn't bad. He even used the correct forms of "to lie," which was almost unheard of in Texas. Someone had taught him that. His rich homosexual uncle in Hawaii, I supposed, the one who taught him to lisp too. After living with his uncle, he spent two and a half years in jail for credit card fraud, nineteen to twenty-one. That was when he learned to be sexually patient. That was where he learned he never wanted to rape anyone. He showed me scars on his shoulder, his wrists, and his abdomen. As he held up his top, exposing his well-toned abdomen, he looked at me seductively.

I couldn't believe this guy. I said dryly, "Yes, those are really nice abs. Thanks for showing me."

He laughed and rolled his shirt back down slowly. "Yeah, you're pretty smart."

Finally, I decided to go to bed. It might be better for Dad to have quiet than to listen to this man trying to chat up his daughter.

"Hal? He's awake, if you want to talk to him."

"I'll be right there," I replied automatically, not knowing where I was or whose voice I was answering. I sat up and felt around on the floor for my glasses. My head cleared a bit. Dad's office. The male nurse.

"I tried to wake Candice," said Thomas as I came into the hall, "but she wouldn't budge."

"He's awake!? Is he talking?"

"Yeah!" said Thomas. "That wasn't a coma, just a real deep sleep."

Dad was sitting up on the edge of the bed trying to raise himself, or trying to pull out the catheter. He looked up at me, sad and surprised.

"Hi, Dad," I said putting my arms around him. "You're awake!" I looked at Thomas and mouthed, "He thinks he has to go."

"If he wants to get up, we should let him try."

We each took an arm. My cheek was pressed against my father's, supporting his head as we lifted him, but he didn't have the strength to stand on his own, so we lowered him gently down again.

"Let him sit up if he wants to. It's good for him," said Thomas. "It's going to seem like you need to go to the bathroom, Mr. MacDonald, but you have a catheter. It takes care of it."

Dad still seemed confused.

"Show him how it works," I said. "I'll leave the room for a minute. Thomas, you tell him." I went out in the hall and when I came back in again, Dad had calmed down a bit. Or he seemed at least to have accepted his predicament.

I sat down next to him. He tried to speak, but had forgotten about his trachea operation. I put my hand over the tube for him.

"Who is this guy?" he asked in that weird strained voice, thumbing at Thomas.

"He's a nurse, Dad. You're not going to the hospital. We're keeping you at home, so you can have twenty-four hour care."

Dad thumbed at the door. "Get him out of here."

"Dad, we need a nurse."

He yanked at his feeding tube.

"Stop that," I cried. "Nobody's feeding you. Nobody's making you go to the hospital, but we need a nurse to keep you comfortable. I'm going to wake up Candice, okay?"

Before I could get very far down the hall, I heard Tommy call my name. I hurried back into the bedroom and found that Dad's feeding tube had been pulled out. He was now lying with his eyes closed. The tube that had been yanked from his stomach lay on the bedside table. The bulbous end was bloody.

"Daddy!"

"Sometimes they do that," said Thomas holding my shoulders. "It's not necessarily intentional, like a drowning man, they just grab."

"Oh Dad, why did you do that? I'm going to need it to give you medicine," I whispered. He opened his eyes and looked blankly at the ceiling. He looked a little like he might cry. "I'm sorry," I said, kissing his hand. He felt a little feverish and his hair was sweaty. I brushed it back. "We want to make you comfortable, that's all."

Thomas examined the incision. "It'll close up pretty quick. I'll clean it up, but I don't think I'm going to be able to get the tube back in. The end is too big. He might have to go to the hospital to replace it."

"No, he doesn't want to go back to the hospital. We promised."

"He can't eat without it." Thomas paused. "I know what." He picked up a piece of small tubing that went with the respiratory equipment. "I'll at least be able to give him medicine with this, some liquids."

When he was finished, I asked Thomas to wait outside the door. I sat down on the bed and Dad opened his eyes and smiled weakly.

I showed him the new tube in his stomach. "I need this to give you your medicine. Do you understand me Dad? No one is going to try to feed you, so don't take it out. Dad, I need it. Do you hear me Dad? I'm here to do what you asked me to do, but you have to leave the tube alone. No one is going to torture you. Can you wait a little because your brother is on his way?"

His hands relaxed. He nodded and closed his eyes. I lay down next to him and, after a while, I fell asleep.

When I woke at seven, Thomas was sitting cross-legged in a chair at the foot of the bed. "What time is it?" I asked.

He pressed his lips together and stared at me without speaking. After a while he finally said, "Time for me to go."

The day nurse arrived, Irma. She was a large woman with red hair, not very knowledgeable, it seemed. Still, Dad preferred any woman nurse to Thomas. Dad remained awake now, and he even pretended to flirt with Irma, pumping his eyebrows when she changed his pajamas.

Later that afternoon, I found Irma sleeping in her chair. She stirred, apologized, and explained that she usually worked nights. I asked her if she would like to work the night shift instead, since Dad didn't like Thomas. I tried calling the nursing association, but the switch couldn't be arranged, and we were to expect Thomas's return that evening.

Irma spent the rest of the day in the TV room talking on the phone to her family while Candice kept an eye on her husband. Annie, Molly, and Molly's husband took off from work. Candice's own kids arrived from far away with their kids, wives, and boyfriends. We all sat around the kitchen, the bed, or the patio talking aimlessly. Meanwhile, Dad had a steady stream of visitors wishing him good-bye. Old friends, neighbors, and clients marched in and out. Dad let them speak. He didn't try to answer. But he did open his eyes every now and again, and he smiled for them. My mother made an appearance and stood at the foot of his bed, looking like a nervous cat. Dad tried to appear reposed already and happy, to make her feel better.

Neighbors contributed food. There was an endless supply of ham and pasta salads. At the end of the day, Dad was worn out but restless. The doctor suggested a suppository tranquilizer, which, he warned us, might put him into a sleep from which he wouldn't wake. We would give it to him when (and if) we were ready. We decided to wait until Uncle Scott arrived.

In the late evening finally, Annie and I were able to be alone with him. He tried to speak. I covered his trachea tube. He said, "It didn't work."

We weren't sure we had heard right. He didn't seem coherent.

"What didn't work, Dad?" asked Annie. She tried to help him speak, but he couldn't muster enough energy. His hand fumbled with the tube. "Bad dreams."

I told him I was sorry to make him hang on, but that his brother was on his way from New Mexico. He tried to speak again and managed to say clearly, "Let's wait."

XXIII

I DON'T WANT to act alone, Dad. You thought I would be strong enough. I am not. One cannot be singled out by a father when there are two other daughters. One does not want to feel special in the ethical-moral universe. One wants to go with a wave of action that binds and unites sins and kindnesses.

I want to tell my sisters about the suicide manual and the trip you and I took to the store for the amber bottle. I want to tell them about the way you pulled me aside and asked me to help. They will not be surprised. Like me, they expect you to want to get it over with without a lot of pain.

We sat on the patio, in the perfume of a citronella plant. Moss rose grew between the cracks of the terracotta tile. It reminded me of my terrace in southern France. Dad and Candice called it "little Santa Fe" after their favorite spot.

"He said he had a bad dream," said Annie, looking beyond the park.

I didn't want him to have any more.

That night the treatment that Thomas gave Dad was rough. He writhed in pain as Thomas put the tubing twice as far down his throat as any of us ever had. His eyes stared. Then Thomas jiggled it around while Dad gaped with a look of horror. I stood by the bedside cringing, but this time I didn't interfere.

When Thomas was done, Dad began to breathe perfectly smoothly. His face relaxed, and he slept. I decided to take a nap curled up at his feet. Dad smiled and stroked my head with his toe.

Thomas took his place in the chair at the foot of the bed. "I let you tell me what to do last night, but not tonight. Now he's better."

"You're right," I said. "You didn't explain it to me. I didn't realize how much better he would feel."

"You asked the association to replace me. Hey, don't worry. It's cool. Happens all the time. A lot of people don't like me at first. Hey, I bet Irma sat around watching TV all day, right? At least I take care of my patient."

"Thank you."

"Hey, I wasn't looking for that. Why are you so cold?"

I laughed. "Am I?"

"You answer questions with more questions."

"I'm going to make some coffee. Want some?"

Thomas followed me to the kitchen. I sat down and said, "I don't mean to be evasive. I'm just tired."

"What is your book about?"

"The one I wrote?"

"Yeah, the one you wrote. You're doing that on purpose now. I noticed it on the shelf."

"A back-sliding atheist."

"Is anyone really an atheist? You have to believe in something. Even if it's only the Big Boom."

You've just made yourself significant, Thomas. "You mean the Big Bang," I said. "No, I don't believe the Big Boom is God or Spirit or anything like that. We mistake the sorting actions of time and chance for divine intention."

"You didn't tell me you were married."

"Did you need to know that in order to care for my father?"

"The book jacket said you were married to a painter. What kind of painter is he?"

"He is the greatest living painter. There is only one every century or two. I am married to him."

"And you didn't mention it. And you aren't wearing a wedding band."

"What do you call this?"

"It's silver. That's not a wedding band. At least it doesn't look like one."

"It's platinum."

"Can I see it?"

I handed him the ring.

"See how easily I got you to take it off," he said with a vulgar smile. "Heavy. I bet you two decided to get silver rings so that it wouldn't look like you were wearing wedding bands. Oh, Tiffany's. Nice. Is that the kind of marriage you have? Kind of casual?"

"It isn't an ordinary marriage."

"He lose interest in you? Show me the most beautiful woman in the world, and I'll show you a man who is tired of fucking her."

"No he didn't. It's my fault. I work too much." *Just like my father.*

"'Cause those rich guys, you know, tend to put their women up on the auction block every five years or so. I wouldn't get tired of you." He waited for my reaction. Not getting one, he laughed, then showed me the best angle of his face. "I'm just playing with you."

"Why don't we see how my father is doing?" I suggested.

At six the next morning Thomas was waking me again. I had fallen asleep next to Dad, and he was now sitting up next to me, wanting to talk. His eyes were wide, and he smiled like his mother's "Davey." He tried to speak and was again surprised and confused that he had no voice. I covered his trachea tube for him.

"What's wrong with me?"

"You have can—," I started to say but checked myself. "You had cancer, but you went to the hospital. Now you're okay."

"What hospital?"

"Presbyterian. Don't you remember?"

He shook his head. "Were there long bright hallways? It was cold."

"Yes, but don't worry. You're not going back. You're okay now."

He reached out and brushed my cheek with his hand, and then pulled me towards him and kissed me all over my face, smiling like a little boy.

When Candice came in at seven I told her he didn't remember anything about the cancer. I was so grateful. "I told him he is going to be okay!" I said.

I would be gatekeeper. Visitors must not cry. Visitors must pretend he is going to be okay.

Now is my chance. A beautiful day. He is happy.

I gave him enough morphine to keep him sleepy and withdrew to my room. Candice lay in bed with him all afternoon, stroking his hair and kissing his cheek. He was too drugged to speak, but he smiled. He petted Charlie, the poodle, who lay at his feet. Uncle Scott arrived and was surprised to find his baby brother out of the coma. They sat together enjoying fraternal silence. Now is my chance.

"I just couldn't let that old bastard do that anymore to him," Uncle Scott was saying to Molly. "I couldn't stand to see Davey hurt." He was sitting now in the nurse's chair facing the bed. Dad was sleeping. "He was a small boy, really small. He never spoke back. He loved his mother. Why did the man have to beat him so hard? He couldn't have been more than four." Scott cried a little. Molly waited, and he went on. "I broke the old man's nose one day, and some of the furniture in the house. That's when I left for good for the Navy. Had to."

"Dad doesn't give up much of his early history," said

Molly. "He only says that his father was 'strict.' Sometimes he says 'mean.'"

"Oh he was mean, all right. He was a mean son-of-a-bitch."

After a while, Dad woke long enough to gaze dumbly at Scott, who had put on his uniform for the occasion. He must have seemed like a dream to him to see his half-brother in uniform, twelve years his senior, his hero in war, a navy captain in peace, his idol, his friend, his fatherly brother.

The last day. The last day, a beautiful day, I thought as I listened to Uncle Scott and Molly. *What mercy that he should have forgotten that he is dying. Now is my time, while he is happy and thinks tomorrow he will walk the dog. The leaves are turning, and the weather will be fine.*

I was in my Dad's office when Annie came in with an empty amber bottle and a prescription vial marked "Demerol" in her hand. She had found it on his bathroom counter. The amber bottle was the one Dad and I had bought together.

"Candice said he got up in the middle of the night," said Annie. "She found him a few hours later in the TV room unconscious. That's what he must have meant when he said, 'It didn't work.' That must have been why he had bad dreams. He tried to kill himself," she cried. "He's been so confused for the past week or so. I don't think he could have known what he was doing."

I took the empty bottles from Annie. "I wonder how much was in them," I mumbled. *I should have tried to get some barbiturates in New York. You're supposed to mix the drugs. That's what the book says. But I stalled. I was hoping it wouldn't be necessary.* "You know, if he took all this, he must have a high tolerance. The little doses we've been giving probably aren't doing anything for the pain. Poor Dad! I wondered why his face has been twitching.

"We've got to tell the nurses without letting Candice find out," I said to Annie. "I don't want her to know what he did all alone like that."

I found Irma in the TV room and told her my father had probably tried to commit suicide. I told her what he had taken. I asked her what *would* kill someone who had survived what he had survived. I didn't care what she thought. I supposed that all hospice nurses understood this kind of thing.

Irma said that the liquid tranquilizers we had on the table would probably do it, but then she told me that her grandfather had tried to kill himself with morphine and barbs when he had cancer, and he had failed. "He hung on for ten months after that. Everyone has their time," she said. "And nobody but God can decide. Your Dad got his message."

I smiled at her faintly, regretting my mistake. She turned back toward the violent program she had been watching.

"We'll have to give him extra morphine to stop the pain. He's obviously built up a high tolerance."

Irma agreed.

"But don't tell Candice. She doesn't need to know what he did. Besides, Irma," I said, "I don't really know anything. I merely assume. I could be wrong."

XXIV

THE SUN IS so bright you can hide in its blinding light. The hot rough concrete feels good under my bare feet. Four laps, six laps, ten laps, then I go out of the park, running down the side of the parkway, under electrical Eiffel towers. Turning my forty-five minute tape over for the second time. The same tape I listened to in France over and over again. It feels good to push my body. I start to sprint down a long asphalt stretch. I can feel my heart pounding and sweat gets in my eyes.

I try not to think what it was like for him, sitting there in front of the dammed TV, knowing he was dying. What was on? some idiotic program? What was he thinking? Did the morphine help him not think or care? or did it make his fear even more large and monstrous? And when he woke, was that fear relieved with a grateful sigh?

Seth had not let me wallow in it. He was jealous of the time that I spent on my father. "Can you help me write about my father's death?" he had asked. "He was ill for so long. I think I should use the idea of assisted suicide in my paintings of my father. I wouldn't do it for my father, you know. I don't think it's right."

Singularities are linked to mental breakdown. The point at which an unpredictable new structure evolves. I think I remember reading there is universality to mental disorders, just as there is a universality to cloud formations. But remaining locked in a single mode can be death. A little chaos is "a health." Flexibility prevents breakage. Thomas says I must bend or else I will break.

When I returned from my run at six, I burst through the door to Dad's office, disturbing Thomas and Irma in a conference. They looked at me guiltily. Thomas seemed angry or disappointed, as if I had slighted him. I looked him in the eye: *everything is true; pity me; help me; I'll love you if you do.*

Thomas stared at my face. I was flushed from the heat and breathing hard. Then he stepped back and looked at me. My hair was in pigtails, and I was wearing a Cat-in-the-Hat shirt Dad had found for me in the boys' section at K-Mart. Thomas' expression went from shock and jealousy to pity. Irma watched us looking long and hard at each other. Thomas started to speak. "I..." then he shook his head and said instead, "You look like a kid." *You're just a little kid without your high heels, your make-up, your stockings, and your fancy words.*

"Excuse me. I didn't mean to interrupt," I said, backing out, and closed the door.

Later, I found Thomas smoking on the patio alone. He gave me one.

"I don't smoke much, but it's a good excuse to talk to you in private."

Why trust Irma? he asked. Why not him? Huh? He had dreamt I would ask for his help. He had dreamt it. He was coming to me tonight with that dream in his mind.

"I was afraid you would get too involved," I said. "I just wanted information."

"Don't ever trust weak people!" he said. "Weak people will mess you up. Irma can already see herself on Oprah talking about how you did a Kevorkian on your Dad. A rich girl like you, good-looking. They would love to get your ass on video. And Irma wouldn't sell you out just for the money. No, she wants her fifteen minutes. Let me tell you about weak minds," he went on. "When they have a secret, they tell it. It doesn't matter what. You thought she was stupid and you could pick her brain, use her for what you want, then ignore her. Never ignore the weak ones. They'll hurt you."

"You're right," I said. I was thinking of my mother. (And he had been thinking of his mother, I could tell.)

"You're not a good judge of character. Why didn't you come to me? I've helped your father. Didn't he breathe better last night?"

"Don't you remember I asked about the Dilaudid?"

"Yes, I do. And I said to myself, what's up with that? Now I know."

"You just supposed I was interested in it for my own use."

"I was just feeling you out. So tell me."

"My father took an overdose of morphine and Demerol on Wednesday night."

"I *thought* that coma of his was strange!"

"I've known he was planning this since the summer. I helped him hide the drugs. But he told me he wanted me to give him the lethal dose. He didn't want to die in pain, 'crapping all over himself,' is what he said. He made me promise. If I hadn't promised, he would have blown his head off. He'd already cleaned his gun and bought bullets. I promised."

Thomas said my dad must trust me an awful lot to have chosen me to help.

"He knows I'll do it. What does that say about me?"

"He knows you're logical."

"Yes, logical. That's what I am." *It made me cry. And logical people are unpoetical, Dad once said. But this one has doubts and fears.*

"He's never asked for help from anyone. Why me?"

Thomas said, "Because you're his baby girl."

I was stunned by the beauty of his statement. It meant nothing and everything.

"What kind of help do you need? You only have to ask, Hal. Ask." He looked away and added softly and ironically, "I'm just a drifter from a small East Texas town. I have nothing to lose."

"Information is all I really need. I know he must have taken a massive dose, and it didn't kill him. What kind of mixture would be lethal to someone with his tolerance? I don't want to screw up. He expects me to do it well." I paused. "Maybe you can give him the suppository tranquilizers the doctor prescribed, since Dad would not want me to do that. I will do the rest. I don't think he remembers that he asked me to do this for him since he doesn't seem to remember the last six months at all—or his cancer. Thank luck. But if he does remember, he won't suspect I'm doing it if you or one of my sisters is in the room with me. We'll tell him it's medicine to help ease his breathing."

It was decided, then. I would get Annie to stay after everyone had gone to bed. I would tell her I planned to give him enough tranquilizers to make him go into a coma till he died. I would tell her we didn't want him to have any more bad dreams, and she would agree. I would dress for bed myself. Thomas and I would administer the dose at eleven, wait for Dad to fall asleep, and Annie would go home around eleven thirty, before he passed away.

Jack and Molly were going to the opera that night. It was their anniversary. She stopped by in her gown on the way to say good-night to Dad. I wanted to, but didn't tell her. Then she went away, like a princess to a ball, leaving him full of pride and dear heartache to see her go.

Now the sound of a clock ticking. Thomas sat at the table facing the stained glass lamp that hung in the center. His skin looked warm and smooth. Annie sat to his left. I sat across the table from him, knowing the light would be as kind to my face, and I tilted it up to keep the shadows from falling the wrong way. We looked at each other for a while, saying nothing. Thomas told a story about swimming the river near Uncertain, Texas, where Dad and Candice had visited and where Thomas had spent summers as a child. Annie and I had never been. Was it in bayou country? I asked softly, focusing on his eyes. Yes, it was. He paused.

Then Thomas said, *You are a beautiful woman. I am a green-eyed boy,* in French. Then he laughed, "That's the only French I know. You speak it, don't you?"

I told him no.

Now I hesitated. I could not bring myself to say, It's time; let's do it. The clock went twelve. It was my responsibility to say, *now,* set the plan in motion. But then Thomas got up.

"C'mon," he said.

I obeyed. Annie and I started to follow him down the long hall to Dad's bedroom. "Annie, get some cough medicine for me," he said. "Hal, you come with me." We went into my dad's room. "Get that Dilaudid for me, girl," said Thomas. With that I was equated with Annie, she and I merely following orders. Let him take control. Tell me what to do. I handed him the pill bottle from the nightstand. He took it, looked me in the eye as he did so, and then left the room.

A few minutes later he returned from the kitchen with a wineglass filled with pink liquid. He was stirring it with a needle-less syringe. Annie came in with a bottle of Nyquil and set it on the nightstand. We took our places in the dimly lit bedroom. Only a small yellow light by the bedside was used because Dad's eyes were sensitive, perhaps from the morphine. A little after midnight now. The house was so quiet but for Charlie, who was snoring noisily next to Dad. He smiled in his sleep.

"Ready?" asked Thomas.

Annie panicked. She said in tears, "Do you think we should? Is it right?"

I answered with a necessary lie, then told Annie to go sit on the other side of the bed. She did.

Now Dad. Here we are. What shall I say as last words? Do you remember talking to me about immortality, just the other day? How we can see light from stars that are ten billion light years away and that might not exist anymore? Do you remember?

You said, The night sky might be filled with ghosts. And I said, But they're real to us. So maybe if people see you everywhere and think you exist, then you do.

"He is sleeping so peacefully," said Annie, recovering a little.

"All right, now . . ." said Thomas, and tapered off.

Dad, I must do this quickly now, without stopping for thoughts or tears, if I can. We will cry later, forever maybe, but we must not now.

I pulled the tube free from Dad's pajama top. His eyes sprang open. Annie put her hand on his arm. I said softly. "Hi Dad. You're awake. Annie and I are here."

He smiled.

"Hi Dad." Annie stroked his cheek.

"I'm going to give you a little medicine to help you breathe more easily, Dad."

He smiled again. He never looked so like a little boy.

"You're doing so much better today, Dad. You're going to be okay. You know that, don't you?"

He nodded.

I took the syringe from Thomas.

"Someone has to hold the tube," he said. Annie was holding Dad's hand, so Thomas took the tube himself. The syringe was difficult to push, so he helped. The cold fluid gave Dad an immediate rush. His eyes fluttered.

Never would he suspect that his daughter planned a quiet death for him tonight. I was smiling at him. I didn't seem sad. He didn't suspect. Everything was too perfect for him to die. I was happy that I had let Molly go off to the opera in a shimmering white gown, with her blonde ringlets piled on her head, enveloped in warm perfume. *That is an image of our future without you, Dad. Look at it while you die and be at peace. Molly has gone to the opera.*

She has left me in charge. Did I mind? she had asked. Was it wrong to go? she had wondered.

No, go to the opera. Have a good time, I had said, thinking, *Let him think of you as going to the opera in a shimmering white gown forever. Die happy, Daddy. Without fear. We will be okay.*

Thomas left us alone. Annie and I sat on either side. Dad was fully awake now. I cozied up against him, singing, "Way out here they have a name for wind and rain and fire. The rain is test; the fire is joy, and they call the wind Mariah." Annie said I had a good voice. I smiled. It wasn't true.

I kissed his forehead. He smiled. Did he really know? Was he just pretending not to? Maybe. But if so, he would also know how gently I was hiding the fact that I had just given him a lethal dose. He would be able to hang on to a belief in his life till the end. I told Dad about the beautiful fall weather that was coming. "And the plans Candice has for you!" He smiled. "Santa Fe, shopping in the bazaars. You better add another leaf to your dining table for all the new candlesticks."

"Remember when we used to hold chocolate ice cream pow-wows telling bedtime stories?" asked Annie. I was three; Annie four; Molly five, with messy faces and tablespoons big as ladles in our little hands. "Remember your names for us? Molly was Snaggle Tooth, because of her missing teeth. I was Fizzlebritches." Annie closed her eyes, laughing in embarrassment.

"And I am still Snakes-in-Hair."

"And Dad was Big Chief Bumble Butt."

He smiled, tried to speak. I quickly covered his trachea tube. He said something about, "playing Noah," or "we know a . . ." something about his brother Scott, but he became exhausted and couldn't go on. We didn't press him.

Annie smoothed his hair and told him how handsome he looked. He pumped his eyebrows, but then his eyes fell, and the drugs plunged him into sleep. His breath deepened. Annie and I looked at each other and swallowed hard, listening to the distant clock chiming the half-hour.

"Goodnight Dad. See you in the morning."

"You should go on home now," I said to Annie.

"You sure? You'll be okay?" she cried.

"Yes, I'm sure." Show no doubt. "He'll be fine. He'll just be in a deep dreamless sleep."

We got up gingerly. Thomas met us at the front door.

I hugged Annie in the dark doorway. *She had his raincloud colored eyes.* I wish she could have stayed. But now I would be alone with my father, having done finally what he wished me to do.

As I watched Annie drive away, Thomas took my chin in his hand and said sternly, "Nothing happened. Do you hear me? No one speaks. No one knows."

I resented Thomas' anger and didn't respond. Instead I returned to Dad's bedside. In his sleep now he seemed unconscious. *I lied to you, Dad, said your cancer has been cured and tomorrow you will walk the dog. The leaves are turning, and the weather is fine.* He sucked long hard breaths, and each one was several seconds apart. I lay down carefully next to him. He would feel my hand on his arm when he died. He would feel warmth. No voices, no thoughts, no actions to trouble him. No priests, no prayers, no good-byes. In the ordinary quiet, we would sleep through death.

Then Thomas came in. "I want to talk to you," he said. I followed him to the living room. He made me sit on the sofa

152

next to him. He stared at me intensely for a long time. "It was heavier than I thought it would be." He looked angry. He ran his hand over his cropped head. *"I need a fucking joint,"* he said, emphasizing every word. "I had to go out and smoke three cigarettes back to back."

"I know," I said, trying to imagine. I had thought it would be horrible, but for me it hadn't been. It had been almost lovely; I hadn't had to do it alone. The act was sanctioned. Done without making my father face death directly. He was sleeping peacefully. "I'm sorry you got involved. It was wrong."

"Damn it, girl." He got up suddenly and went out on the porch to have another cigarette. Through the window, I could see that he had turned to watch me follow. I did, slowly.

"It's chilly," he said.

I was in my slip, feet bare. He handed me his cigarette and lit another for himself, then looked at me sideways.

"Do you know how close you came to getting caught out by Irma? You going to be that messy with me? It was right what we did, but I put my career on the line."

I exhaled and said, "My dad."

He nodded. "You know," he said, "I told you I had a dream yesterday that you would ask for my help. Man! What is going on?" He stamped out his cigarette early. "I have to check on my patient. My patient. Do you hear me? The man I am responsible for."

I followed him back to the bedroom and stood by the bedside, watching now as Thomas checked my dad's breathing and pulse.

Dad overestimated me, thinking I could do this without involving others. Pale girl sleeps while man strokes his ginger beard and stares, thinking. I feel my body begin to throb. The adrenaline. The rush of death. The kind warm light, the quiet. Thomas got sucked into it. I saw it happening and I let him get sucked into it.

Dad knew. 'Who is this guy? Get him out of here.' He had pointed to the door. He instinctively knew.

I took Dad's limp hand and knelt beside the bed. I could feel Thomas standing behind me. "You're like a porcelain doll," said the invader to the king's daughter. I lay down and closed my eyes. Thomas sat by the bed watching.

Dad's breaths began to come further and further apart. At three AM they became very shallow. I was finally put to sleep by the slow rhythm of death, but some time later I half woke up. In the dimness of the shadows, stupid from the drug of sleep, I saw a vision of Thomas injecting something into Dad's stomach tube. Gently and expertly he capped the tube and replaced Dad's pajama top. Thomas looked like a nurse, a professional. He looked like he knew what he was doing. He seemed to have overcome his misgivings and resumed control of himself and the situation. I felt euphoric. I had been relieved of the charge. Then Thomas glanced at me and was surprised to find me staring at him.

"I'm hydrating him, to make him comfortable," he explained.

I continued to look in his anxious green eyes. He read my look. I saw shock and a little humility cross his face. He wasn't going to let himself believe it. I looked at him steadily until he finally had to turn away and leave the room.

I noticed that Dad's sleep was still deep, but his breathing had become more regular, and when I brushed his hair back, he seemed to be able to feel it. It wasn't working.

I sat at the kitchen table. Thomas came up from behind and stood there for a while, and his thoughts seemed to press against my back. Eyes on my neck. Then he sat down beside me and sighed. He said the dose we had given him wasn't enough.

I said that I would give him another dose, and it would be that one that would actually cause his death. Thomas would stay out of the room this time. That way he could not be held responsible. "I would be the only one!"

This made Thomas angry. "I thought you were smart, but your logic's way off," he laughed. "If I gave him another dose without your knowledge would that take the responsibility from you?"

"No," I said, slow to realize.

"I just gave him another dose. A big one."

I left my chair and put my arms around him. His body stiffened. His arms remained rigid at his sides. I kissed him on the temple. Then I stepped out of the embrace. "Poor us," I said softly.

We returned to the bedroom. The second dose was taking effect. I got back in bed with my father, and Thomas stood by watching. "I need to touch your face."

I shook my head.

He said I wasn't so complicated. It was all a front. I was really simple after all, he said.

"Too simple," I answered.

Had someone else done what he did, I would love him too. It was a simple reaction. I was worn out and afraid. I let him hold me when we went out into the yard to smoke. After what he had done, anyone would understand. Anyone. The house was dark. Everyone was sleeping. He had dreamt of helping me. He had spent the night before watching me sleep next to my dying father. And he couldn't believe how pale I was.

"I'm grateful for your courage where mine failed," I said, but I was thinking, *No, it was desire, not courage, that made you do what you did.*

This time he pressed himself up against me. Dad's nurse. His arms were hard. *We are thinking in adrenaline. No one will blame me. I am not myself. I will never be again. I want to be weak . . . No, I don't want to be like my mother.*

I pulled away, and he said, "I won't move till you tell me to."

Months of working out an understanding of death, all the words, all the ideas had vanished. Now there was this gap. I looked around. Nothing but shivering fetal emotion waiting for someone to flesh it out.

"I can't," I said.

"I understand," he said and stepped back.

"I mean I can't say it," I said weakly.

"You don't need to say another word. I know exactly what you want."

Unstoppable now. I'd spoken words to Mephisto that I couldn't call back because I'd spoken by not speaking. That's how he gets you.

I ran into my Dad's office and called Seth at his studio. "April is here with me, and I'm getting a really good drawing. I better get back to work."

"I feel like I'm in a little lifeboat," I said, crying. "In the middle of the ocean. I would climb onboard any ship that came by."

"Halibut," he said, "sweet Tender-Halibut. That's such a sweet image."

"Oh go back to work," I said and hung up, but then I picked up the phone and immediately redialed.

"I am not weak! Forget that I called! I didn't mean to let you see me like that. Forget it."

"Do you want me to come down right now or wait till Thanksgiving?"

"No! Don't come at all till the funeral. The house is crowded. There's nowhere for you to sleep. There is a nurse here who is going to tell me what to do."

"Well, maybe it's better to let the nurse help. They do this kind of thing all the time."

XXV

I woke when I heard Thomas straightening up the bottles on the nightstand. This is fighter's syndrome, he said. It was six AM. Dad had begun to recover again. "He is not metabolizing the drugs. His body is in shock, and it's not absorbing anything. Months of chemo and morphine did it." Thomas had never seen it like this.

Irma would be arriving any minute. Did I have that Demerol? "Give it to me," he said loudly enough for my father to hear.

"Yes, I think I know where it is," I said. "I'll go get it."

Dad didn't even respond, this time, to the injection. "He's tired," I said. "He must be so tired." I lay down again and immediately fell asleep.

"You see this?" It was Thomas waking me up again, showing me the morphine bottle that we had used up on Dad. "Water. Knock it over in front of Irma. Nod if you understand me." I nodded. Then he held the bottle of cherry Nyquil next to the wine stain on the sheet. I didn't understand. He said, "Look. Think. He had congestion. Got it?" I nodded. "Don't forget about the morphine. Irma will be here any second, and I have to go."

At eight I woke to find Candice smiling down at me. "Did you stay with him all night?"

"Yeah. I fell asleep."

Dad was lying in the same position as he had before.

"He's been very quiet like that for hours," I whispered.

"He looks peaceful," she whispered back. "He doesn't seem to be in any pain. Go to my bed now honey. You need more sleep."

157

Irma had arrived, but instead of doing as Thomas had said, I followed Candice's suggestion. It would all be over soon, and all that stuff Thomas said about the bottles and hiding the drugs wouldn't matter, I thought, climbing into Candice's bed, which was still warm with her perfume.

At eleven-thirty Candice woke me again. She was frazzled. Afraid. So afraid. His breathing was down to three per minute.

"It's time," she said.

It's time. His fingertips and lips were blue. I sat beside him watching him, feeling numb. If I had not done what I had done, then I would have been able to be afraid too. I would have been able to weep and suffer at the sight of my father's body finally becoming unresponsive to touch and sound, but as it was, I could only wait. My weeping and suffering had come before, in Les Monèdes and in my imagination.

So it was working, finally. Of course it was working. He was just a human being, after all. Dad's face winced a little. Now there were two morphine bottles on the table. Which one was filled with water? "He's feeling a little pain," I said, and picked up one of the bottles and gave him a few drops under his tongue. I waited to see if there was a reaction. I couldn't tell.

I didn't want to see him die. I wanted Candice to be the one to stay with him. She could hold his hand as he went over the precipice. I had already let go. I suggested that she read him the poems he'd written to her. He'd told me that they were his best work. I thought he would want to hear them as he died in the voice of the one who loved him best. I left her alone with him, and from the carpeted hall I could hear her reading them softly, reading them well and without tears.

Uncle Scott put on his uniform, and the family gathered. Annie took off from work. Molly came with her family. We watched his body as it stiffened and struggled to take its last breath. The breath slowly leaked out, then nothing. We waited. Then suddenly the vacuum itself would draw in another breath. Air seemed to move in and out of his body without his help, like waves advancing and retreating.

Who around the bed is most free? I wondered. The more one conforms to the predictions and supplies the justifications for the collective action (or non-action in this case), the less one may call oneself free. Whereas the desire to change, control, the course of events makes one free. Like me, free as a bird caught in a wind tunnel.

Irma declared that Dad was in "hills and valleys"; sometimes he had eight breaths per minute, sometimes two. "But that doesn't necessarily mean he will die soon," she went on. Her grandfather, she said, had taken four breaths per minute for five days.

She talked loudly, not caring that Dad might hear. He was "in the process of dying," she said, and she told us what he was feeling as he was dying, what we would see when he died, and what he would look like when he was dead.

They say that hearing is the last thing to go, I whispered.

He seemed to be in pain. I was worried that the bottle we were using was filled with water. Even if Candice was giving him morphine, she didn't know his unbelievable tolerance level. He grimaced. He sweated. His sleep was disturbed. He was having bad dreams.

"We should give him more morphine!" I said.

No, said Irma, too much will kill him. And this made Candice cry.

He's having nightmares! He's having nightmares! I knew it and looked to Annie for help. By her expression I saw she had the same fear. She got Irma and Candice out of the room on some frail pretext. I quickly injected five ounces of

Lorazepam elixir into his stomach. I tasted the liquid in one of the morphine bottles. It wasn't water. I gave him several drops of that by mouth, and I tossed the bottle filled with water open on the carpet. I took the Lorazepam bottle with me out of the room.

An hour later Irma reported an appreciable drop in blood pressure. We rushed from the kitchen table back to the bedroom. Candice hadn't stopped crying. With pretty blue eyes awash, "Breathe, Davey, breathe," she kept saying.

Irma took Candice aside and whispered something.

Candice cried out loud in astonishment. "You think one of the girls gave him an overdose?" Irma tried to stop Candice from confronting us directly, but Candice would have no secrets.

Brave Annie was quick to confess to having given him three drops on the sly.

"That's enough to kill him," replied Irma. "It's not for you to decide," she said. Then she made out a morphine schedule. All doses had to be recorded. Three drops per hour was the absolute limit.

I continued to give him a dropperful every half-hour. But now I had to work in secret, watch the door. I had to dose him quickly without time for tenderness or ironic regret.

My sisters and I, Jack, and Greg sat around the kitchen table or wandered in the park. We were all like zombies.

"Uncle Scott's a basket case," said Jack. "He can't go on much longer like this." Dave was doubled over by the bed most of the day, recounting stories to anybody who came near. Unreasonable guilt, I supposed, for having left him alone with that horrible man.

But Candice was suffering the most. Dad's beautiful bride wanted him to let go, but she counted the seconds between his breaths, and when one came late, she repeated, Please Davey please, one more.

I suggested the tranquilizers that the doctor had prescribed. Thomas had never given them, I realized. Irma had been pretty sure that they would at least keep him from waking again. "Just to help him sleep," I said.

Molly made an announcement that we, the three daughters, wanted to be alone with our father. As Annie and Molly shut the double doors, I poured the entire bottle of morphine into his tube and more Lorazepam. I would have liked to have been more gentle, more ceremonious, but Irma had left me without emotion. I was dried up as a daughter, unfit for the task. *Families shouldn't have to do this. Where are the doctors? Can't somebody help?*

Annie found a morphine patch. Resourceful Annie. I stuck it behind his knee, where no one would notice it, not right away. Then we rolled him over to put the suppository tranquilizers in. I fumbled with the package. The white bullets fell in the sheets and broke. We heard a noise at the door. Candice stuck her head in the door. We pretended that we had been massaging his back.

"Oh, I'm sorry," she said. "I didn't know you girls were still with him." Candice left, and I said I wanted to try to use the rest of the tranquilizers, to be sure.

"That's enough," said Molly. "We can't do any more. We have to just let it go."

For over six months I dreaded the idea of having to cause his death. And here I am ready to go to any length. I've turned into a zealot. Who was it who said that the perfect plot turns on the idea of a person ending up doing the one thing she wished to avoid most? They would have called that Fate once.

The house is filled with friends and family, sleeping in shifts, eating neighborly ham meal after meal. No one has slept well. *You are still alive, and it's killing us to want it to be over. We can't think it, and we don't want what we want.*

XXVI

INSTEAD OF TAKING cool evening walks around the park with my father and Charlie, I ran obsessively every day in mid-afternoon, around the eight-acre loop, over and over. Then I sprinted.

I look for a message without a sender. I can make sense of anything. In the forest outside of St. Paul Le Jeune, I had followed what seemed to be a human path through the brush, but it may have been a mere gully made by rain converging. I follow a path that may not be a path, thereby making a path.

The neighbors, looking out from their kitchen windows, say, *She's running again. Dave must still be hanging on. Oh that poor family. They must be going crazy.*

I took off my sweaty shirt and lay on the shady lawn in my shorts and halter. The cool thick grass was soothing. I counted out one hundred sit-ups, then I lay there and looked at the sky through the trees. If I looked beyond the park, I could see my sisters in the back yard, sitting around the patio table. I saw my stepbrother also and Jack. I sat up. Something in the situation had changed, I could tell, but I didn't suppose that Dad had died in the time that I had been gone. I lay back down again. The grass was cool.

After a while, I saw that Greg was coming to get me. I sat up and watched him come. When he got within ten feet, he stopped. He said his mother was upset and angry with me because I was giving him extra drops of morphine. And they couldn't find the Dilaudid. Where was the Dilaudid?

Dilaudid? Yes, I think there was some Dilaudid once, somewhere. Did I use it? I must have. Yes, I remember now. Thomas had said, *Get me that Dilaudid*, in a way that had made me uncomfortable. There were bottles of Demerol and

Lorazepam, Morphine, and Dilaudid, lots of stuff. None of it worked. None of it mattered.

"I don't know," I said. "I mean, I don't remember what happened to the Dilaudid."

I'm sorry, Dad, I failed to spare your bride this pain. Should she be told? How important was it to you that she never know? that your gift to her would have been a speedy death right on the heels of great days? that for her you would face the horror of suicide full on? cognizant and frightened, for her? Yes. Perhaps she should know. Love isn't love enough unless it's painful knowledge.

Candice had her role. We had each picked a role to play. Hers was the lover who would cling to the end. She was as brave in her commitment as any of us. None of us was any more right than the other. We all have invented moral scenarios and must act in them accordingly—or lose self-respect. Greg said he had made an attempt to talk to his mother, to get her to let go. But I said no, she doesn't need to change. She's beautiful.

In the hall I met her, and I told her that I loved her.

She hugged me. "I can't let go," she sobbed. "I just can't let go."

I told her not to. "Fight like a tigress for his next breath. He expects that of you."

Suddenly Irma came around the corner and announced in a saccharine voice, "Your Dad's awake!" We turned and looked at her, feeling numb. She stood there smiling perversely.

We went back into the bedroom. Yes, his eyes were open, but he stared blankly. There was nothing in that look. Nothing. *Brain damage*, I thought, *this poor body cannot be him.* Candice propped him up against a stack of pillows and sat next to him, reassuring him that he was home with family, and he wasn't going to the hospital. We rolled him a little on his side so that he wouldn't start developing bedsores. He hadn't yet. Dave MacDonald was a tough old man.

Your eyes are vacant, but you are alive. It's four AM. Dad lives, barely, on. I am exhausted and giddy, and I fall laughing on the kitchen floor. What a mess I have made of this. "Stay away from my butt," he had said, and I had forgotten this one injunction. Dad would be laughing at his Three Stooges.

I'm so sorry Dad. I tried, but it is so difficult to kill you. I imagined one dramatic injection, tears, and quick earnest words. But your death will not come as quickly as you hoped. I'm sorry you're in pain and suffering embarrassment, but you're going and Candice is still here, and as much as I love you, I have to be more concerned with her needs than yours. I do not want to take any more drastic measures.

XXVII

THE NURSING ASSOCIATION called to say that Thomas had already worked forty hours that week and would not be allowed to stay with us over the weekend. Candice slept in bed with Dad, and either Annie or I came in every few hours to give him morphine. Throughout the night, he was recovering from his overdose, and by morning the frozen look on his face had gone. He was able to let his eyes wander around the room, looking merely baffled and confused.

When Candice woke, I left his care to her for the rest of the day. I didn't want him to see me. I passed by the bedroom phantomlike, never making contact, not after that beautiful last good-bye with Annie. I feared that my presence would make him remember that he has cancer, or make him realize that his appointed assassin, sadly willing, is ineffective. Sometimes I would glance in and see that his eyes were open, and on me. I was ashamed. His eyes implored me to come in, but I couldn't.

During the long Sunday afternoon of this long, long weekend I waited for Thomas to return to tell me what to do next. Suzi and Greg were worried that their mom was going to crack up. Dad wouldn't have wanted this. I resolved again to try to do something. I considered the possibility of asking Thomas about an illegal Seconol purchase, and I remembered that Dad had asked for the plastic bag.

"I tried to suffocate him, you know," I said suddenly to Seth, three months later, as we lay in bed.

Seth stirred from half-sleep. "Halibut, I'm sorry." He rolled over and pressed his body against my back.

"I can't sleep. I'm starting to have bad dreams. I feel it now. I wouldn't let myself feel it then. I was like an automaton. I just stood there watching him while he gasped. He kept trying to breathe like a machine that would not be stopped.

"He had said he wanted me to use a plastic bag on him, but I couldn't bring myself to put one over his face. Besides, he had that trachea tube sticking out of his neck. I came up with the idea that I could just snap a balloon over it. I guess I imagined that he would simply re-breathe his own air, get dizzy, fall asleep, and quietly die. But he didn't. He struggled pretty hard."

I started to sob. Seth hugged me. After a while, I laughed a little bit and went on. "I went to the supermarket to get the balloon, and I only could find colorful ones in the party section. It seemed too absurd. I chose a plain white one, as if that would be better somehow.

"If we ever have kids, I don't think I will ever be able to have balloons at their birthday parties," I cried. "I haven't been able to account for that act emotionally, not yet, maybe not ever. I'm scared. I can't remember what I did while his body struggled."

"We won't have balloons at our kid's parties then," said Seth.

"People will wonder. They'll ask questions."

"Then we'll get the foil kind."

"Okay."

He gasped. His eyes sprang open. I removed the balloon and buried my face against his shoulder. His body relaxed again and continued breathing regularly. His eyes fell closed again.

My father told me his wishes. His final words, because final, become frozen in my ears, become madness not open to compromise. Death stops the mind. When the voice no longer speaks, it is law unalterable.

After a while Candice came in to check on him. She found me dry-eyed, staring at the wall. She suggested that I take Dad's car. Get out of the house for a bit. I hadn't been out for—what?—five days now?

I drove aimlessly. If my father died tonight I would not see Thomas again. How strange, I thought, because he seemed so important. Love occasioned or hazarded by the death of my father. I supposed he might come to the wake. Was he watching the obituaries for his chance to meet me one last time? My body ached to see him again. I wasn't thinking anymore. He said he had to struggle to keep himself from touching my pale skin as I lay sleeping next to my father and as he stood by waiting for him to die.

My husband wouldn't help. Morally wrong in my father's case, he had said. And here was one who would cut his own throat for me. I would cut mine too. Two self-destructive puppets alone in a dark house. Everyone asleep and a deed to be done.

I knew it was only a fatigue-euphoria that I had felt on Friday night when he grabbed me and put his tongue in my mouth. I had pulled away, but when I got a few steps down the hall, I had stopped. He'd stood there looking at my bare shoulders in the dim light thinking. He said quietly, *In and out, in and out, you keep going in and out.* I waited for him to move. I wondered if he could see the wet stain on my dark silk slip. I remember thinking how dark and quiet the house seemed with everyone asleep. My nerves seemed exposed. I hadn't slept much. I was cold. He was warm. He walked up and stood in front of me. I put my hand on his chest then, like a blind girl, felt his strong arms and his hard stomach. We could hear our own breath.

I pulled away, went slowly to my father's office and lay down on the floor, pulling a sheet up around me. Thomas, the inevitable nightnurse that I could never have foreseen.

XXVIII

AND THEN THERE was drift.

On Monday afternoon we went for a walk around the park. I told him I loved him for what he had done. I saw his world lurch forward and stagger. But I went on. I had a certain *kind* of love for him. Did he listen? or did the word rush over him in its rich and utter fullness?

I sat down on a park bench at the far end of the park. I watched myself telling him. I watched him listen. It was fascinating. I never meant for either of us to act on the knowledge, only wallow in it.

"Oh come and sit by me anyway—even though you shouldn't." He sat very close to me so that we were both comforted by our warmth. "I feel so sorry for us. It's so predicable. And it can't be helped!" I meant to kiss him gently, as a little more than a friend but not quite a lover, but he grabbed me violently. His loss of self-control was as quick and irrecoverable now as it had seemed perfect days before.

I couldn't let the neighbor see the daughter of the dying embraced by the male nightnurse. I stood up. I put my hand over my mouth. To someone coming down the path I could not explain, not without dragging Freud out of the attic. That kind of absolution appealed to me not at all. I hated to think my actions could be prescribed by a thing called the unconscious.

"Sometimes you scare me, Hal. You're hot and cold. I have to tell you that I almost didn't come back tonight. This shit's on me. I can't *sleep* anymore! I wasn't going to tell you this, but my roommate talked me into going to church with him yesterday. I know. I know how you're going to say that religion is crap."

"I never said religion was crap. It's not that simple."

"Well, anyway. He wants me to talk with one of the deacons who's an attorney."

"What about?"

"I didn't mention who or when or anything, but I said I'd been involved in a situation that could lose me my license."

"What kind of situation?" I asked calmly.

Thomas became agitated. "I'm talking euthanasia, Hal!"

"What exactly did you say?"

"I didn't meet with him yet. I'm going tomorrow. It's something I've got to do for myself."

"Why an attorney? Why a deacon? Religious people are crazy, Thomas. Don't bring those kind of people into this."

"Don't get hysterical. He's a friend of a friend. He's not going to meet with me as an attorney, just as a friend. I'll get some advice."

"What kind of attorney?"

"He's a prosecutor Hal, but I'm just talking to him as a friend."

"Geez, Thomas. Why? He may protect you, but he'll come after me. They'll destroy me here in Texas. Any jury would hate me."

"He said it wouldn't be official."

"Listen Tommy, I understand the need to talk. You should be able to. It shouldn't have to be a secret. People have a right to die. Tell him if you feel you have to. I'll stand by you, say you did the right thing. Or I'll say that you tried to help, but it was I who did it."

"I was the one, Hal. I fucking hate it when you try to deny that I am involved."

"Do me a favor. Don't speak to him for a few days. Give me a chance to warn Seth."

"Don't go telling him anything about me. I don't need a jealous husband knocking on my door."

"Seth's not like that."

"What kind of man is he? Is he a man?" Thomas waited. "You're not going to answer me."

"Dad is quiet tonight," I said after a while. "Maybe you can get some rest too."

"Maybe I can get some," said Thomas, frowning.

I went methodically through the medicine chest and bathroom closet, and I discovered a full bottle of Vicodins. I dissolved them in water. When Thomas came into the bedroom, I said, "Keep them out for two minutes."

"What are you going to do?"

"Don't ask questions." He resisted, so I said, "Do what I say."

Candice was coming down the hall. Thomas left to intercept her.

The dissolved Vicodins were as thick as cream of mushroom soup, but I injected the mix, then flushed the tubing, and was replacing his clothing as Uncle Scott came in the room.

"Still the same?" he asked.

"Yes," I said. "I'll leave you alone with him."

Thomas was now on the patio. He grabbed my arm and pulled me through the gate into the park.

"She asked me pointblank, 'She's not going to overdose him, is she?' She had tears in her eyes, Hal. I didn't want to lie to that woman, but I did. I did it for you." He released my arm with a jerk, pushed me away, then went back into the house.

I found him again later in the kitchen. He whispered at me harshly, "You left a residue trace in his tube. I cleared it out for you. And there was a blockage in his catheter because you didn't use enough liquid with the pills. How many were there? Twenty?"

"Forty."

"Shit."

"I didn't want to involve you again. So I sent you out of the room."

"I just want to protect you. Think, Hal, You're not a stupid girl. Don't put me in a position where I have to lie to Candice about what you plan to do. Besides, Vicodins won't do it if the Morphine and Demerol didn't. He's not metabolizing opiates."

"Well, at least it will keep him from waking."

"I wonder about you," he said. "How can you be so cold?"

They do not see that my control is a kind of madness.

"I can see that little mind of yours working it," he went on. "You use lots of words, words, words, but they never say what you feel."

* * *

Words are the very fibers of my feeling, the nerves of my mind. Space to cry in. The day my father dies, I do not cry. I do not cry when they take his body away or when I go through his papers. It will happen two weeks later in a bookstore when I overhear someone quote Hamlet: "There are more things in heaven and earth, Horatio, than are dreamt of in your philosophy." The first tears spontaneously spring, like magic. I stand in the aisle, soundlessly crying, wiping my nose on my sleeve, feeling as if I had finally stepped into that warm bath of grief.

XXIX

FATHER, AS WE close in around your deathbed, the idea you had of your ending gets away from you. The editors in black descend and tidy up. One wants you to be remembered as a little less flip than you actually were and much less than you seem in your "auto-obit." Another fills up the rituals you found empty. Plans are made for your memorial service, and your last words are revised. Your authorial control slips away. And as the sense of your ending does change, we are left free to reinterpret all that went before.

"I want a cardboard box," I scream. "I want a cardboard box."

I bring a mind to the bedside that might not be changed by its surroundings because it is the tyrant of its *own* place and time. In the mind, necessity loses footing, slides down the slope, clutching at exposed roots.

God's will? or just the way things have worked themselves out?

What do we get now if we give up fate? Do we get a sense of control?

No, look at me. Knowledge is too uncertain for one to act in a timely way. I might have planned better. I might have researched more, but who would have predicted Dad's super-human resistance to drugs?

So death will come in a predictable way. He will starve in eight to twelve days. Taking action, one is less certain what will come. Is that why one stands by? Afraid precious intentions will fall short? overshoot the aim? force one to take responsibility? initiate a complex set of events that no one could have foreseen?

It is true that an intentional act, as opposed to a reaction, is more likely to breed chaos.

And was I just using him? Thomas wanted to know. "What could you possibly want with a punk like me?"

"I didn't mean to make this happen."

"But you made it happen."

"Yes, I made it happen."

"Then you meant to."

"Yes."

"You constantly contradict yourself."

"Then I contradict myself."

Thomas stayed on the next morning after his night shift was done. It was Thanksgiving Day. "It will be today. I finally figured out what he needed. Opiates and tranquilizers wouldn't do it. I mixed his heart medicine with his asthma medicine. He won't last long."

"If only he could hold on one more day," I said. "Then his death would ruin the biggest shopping day of the year instead of Thanksgiving." I half-laughed. "He would like that."

"It's not going to happen," said Thomas. "He will die today."

"When?"

"Within two hours."

"I'm going running," I said. "Don't come to get me. No matter what."

* * *

When you get to the thing itself, you find it vacuous and jumbled, an anticipated stranger at best. The death of your father means nothing to you, and it won't, until it's relived and remembered.

The day before my oral exams, I come down with a fever. As I lie drugged in bed, dozing, I imagine I am he in a daze, dying, frightened, confused, and so lonely. Then I dream of his blue-eyed body, a puppet dressed for a box, and I hear someone's voice wondering which socks to put on his cold feet.

The fever and the dreams delay my exams, but finally I recover, take them, and earn a distinction, but I will not know

174

whom to call with the news. I ride the train home and sit at my desk in an empty house. Who will be proud of me now? For whom will I do things?

My books are closed now. Will I be sick? Visit his widow?

Now will Dad begin to die for me. My thoughts will begin to meet up in a hundred different ways. His relics that now sit on my office shelves—his pipes, his clock, his books—will remind me, over and over, first that he lived, and then that he is dead.

*   *   *

I started out walking, then I sprinted, but it wasn't enough. I wanted to dance or throw a tantrum right there in the park.

Look, there's Dave's daughter in the gazebo. My God, I think she's dancing. How weird. I wonder what happened.

After a while, I felt Thomas coming to get me. It took him a long, long time, from the moment his green scrubs appeared going out of the gate till he slowly came up behind me. I kept dancing. He stood watching. I stumbled. I looked up at him. I couldn't hear him with my Walkman blasting in my ears. But his lips moved, "It's over." I turned off the music and with it went all the feeling.

Dad's body lay alone as he had died. His blue eyes stared. His mouth was open a little. *A man hasn't got an essence, but he has a history, which amounts to the same thing, practically speaking. This is his body. There was a man.* I sat looking at him. The house was quiet. Everyone had retreated to his or her own miserable corner.

After a while, Thomas and Irma came in and stood there like officials. He was not ours anymore. "Can I close his eyes?" I asked.

"Yes," said Thomas.

Irma whispered to him, "They'll just pop back open."

"Let her try," he whispered back.

I closed his eyes with my fingers and held them closed, sitting beside him, looking at his skin, now so smooth. He looked better somehow, even though his head was tilted back and his mouth still open.

I asked Thomas if he would move the body out of its awkward position. He got into the bed next to it and a little above and embraced it, like a wrestler might, with a choke-hold. Then he pushed the remaining air out of the lungs and set the mouth shut and held it there like that. Thomas looked at me lovingly while he waited for the rigor mortis to find and keep the position.

Size is needed. Nurses have to be big and male to shift bodies. "Thanks," I whispered.

An RN came and signed the death certificate. Thomas had told me to tell her I had flushed all the drugs. I did. She noted it down. I was in the bath when I heard the funeral car come and take the body away.

Thomas had poured himself a glass of Wild Turkey. "Let me tell you what to do now," he said. "Make sure you get his body cremated right away. No autopsy can be performed without family consent."

"No one will try. This may be the Bible Belt, but people aren't monsters; they will let it go."

"Protect me. That's all I ask."

"I will."

"Good girl. Now, you've got to give me a little cash for a hotel room. I'm too tired to drive back to Denton. You'll do that for me, won't you?"

I reached for my purse. He said, "Three will cover it."

I handed him the money.

"And then some," he added.

"Tommy, tell me. Did my father's eyes stay closed?"

At first Thomas said nothing; he took a drink, then he lied, "Yes."

* * *

Months later, asleep in a fever, I hear the phone ring. I don't understand what the sound means at first, then I reach for the receiver. It's Tommy again. He calls me every day. He gets angry if I don't answer. I am a slave to the idea that he must get his time with me. He says he has been thinking about my coldness again, wondering how I could have been out there dancing while he was with my father as he died. *He* had cried, he says. I had not.

Then he says he may not be able to work as a nurse anymore. He says someone stole his journal. "It has everything in it, Hal. Everything."

"You kept a journal? Do you mention me?"

"It's all about you."

"Who took it?"

"Doesn't matter who. I have to come up with some cash to get it back." Thomas says I'm his only friend. He says he is in love with me. He needs money. He says he needs to be in New York to be near me, and he wants my help. I tell him I love him for what he did.

"Why do you love me, Hal? Why do you love me?"

"Because you would cut your own throat for me."

"I'm a man, that's why."

"I won't let you, though. I won't let you."

"Buy me a ticket."

"I can't."

"What's five hundred dollars to you?"

"I can let you come, but I can't help."

"Dammit girl, stop pulling my chain."

* * *

Thomas had finished his Wild Turkey and gotten his things together. "I wonder how it will be when it's over, when you won't take my call."

"I'll always take your call."

"You'll wake up one day, and you won't know my punk ass anymore."

"I love you; it can't be helped."

"I want to fuck you," he said. I stared at him as he lit and drew upon a cigarette. "Yeah," he added, then shook out his match and smiled. "And I know you want me to," he went on. "Don't say anything. I know. Your husband coming down tomorrow night?"

"Yes."

"I want to know if you are worthy of what I did," he said.

The words frightened me to death. He picked up his black bag and went to the door.

"Meet me tonight. I'll call you exactly at ten with the address." Then he changed his tone and asked, "Okay?"

"Not your hotel," I answered.

He laughed, "You're that scared of me? or scared of yourself. Tell you what, we'll have a drink."

I sighed, "I shouldn't drink."

"So afraid to lose control. That's exactly what you need—and what you really want. Tell you what: let me take over from here." Laughing, he added, "You even try to control the way you *lose* control. You're a piece of work."

I didn't answer. Instead, I noted that he had unknowingly quoted Hamlet, and I wondered what this could mean, to me.

"Am I right? Isn't that what you want from me?"

You're the male nightnurse, my father's nurse. You are big and strong, and you provide physical comfort to the small and weak or the ill. It's important that you have thick arms and a

178

beautifully curved back, and that you could be so rigid and restrained when your patient's daughter climbs into your lap for warmth. You stare like a demon, and you are probably a better man naked than clothed. You make my mind numb with your egotistical chatter, and all together you're the opiate I've needed.

XXX

I HAVE VOWED to keep Candice away from solicitous funeral directors, who will want only the best for Dave. She will crumble. She'll go for the prettiest blue, the most comfortable box, swayed at last by some horribly inappropriate pitch ("You only go once"), despite my dad's instructions not to waste a dime on his burial. He wanted a pine box, if he had to have one at all, then cremation. No flowers, marker, urn, or fuss. I would see to it. I would defy the oily director, even if I had to make the box myself.

When Scott, Candice, Molly, Annie, and I get to the funeral home, we find that Dad had already purchased his own cheap coffin just weeks before from a discount coffin supplier. Candice says, "That's what he wanted!" She is firm. Laughing-crying, she adds, "That's my Dave."

He also left instructions to scatter his ashes in the backyard where "Charlie buries his bones." But Candice can't do this. She simply can't. "What if I sell the house some, day? I can't just leave him there." She looks at me imploringly. Scott offers to pay for the urn. He wants it for himself, to mix his own ashes in. He too looks to me for consent. But who am I to give or deny it? I smile, showing my sea change, and the urn is purchased.

Candice decides to hold a memorial in a church, although he specifically asked for a wake at the house only. I begin to think that he probably wouldn't have minded if we did it for our own sake, not for his.

He may have wanted a wake, but nothing can force Candice to be happy. She needs to be sad in a church. And so she will have it. Dad, you tyrant! Your power is diminished. People will do what they need to do to make themselves feel better. Let it go. Let it go. Let it go.

XXXI

SETH HAD ARRIVED. "You've lost more weight," he said hugging me. "Cat-in-the-Hat, what's that? You look like a teenaged smack addict. My poor damaged Halibut. You're a wreck." He looked at my face carefully. "But it's kind of sexy."

"I know," I said. I was sitting in my father's office. I had been straightening up his papers, looking at all the funny things he had kept—letters from me, old photos, and newspaper clippings.

"Now you can imagine what I was feeling the day we met, dazed, numb," said Seth. "It will take a long, long time to get over it. When's the funeral?"

"The wake is tomorrow, here. There is a memorial service too at a church before, but I don't think I can stand to hear anybody say 'God's will be done' right now." *Staying through the wake is unthinkable. I have given up my right to cry.*

"What about the nurse who helped you?"

"Tommy."

"The nurse was a man?"

"Yes. Kind of a strange guy from East Texas. You know the type—from a bad home, uses a lot of street talk—but I think he is okay. We went through a lot together. He's nervous. He almost confessed everything to some religious attorney he knows."

"What?"

"He didn't. I calmed him down. I understand how he feels. You have to talk to somebody. You can't be alone in this."

"An attorney? I told you something like this would happen."

"It didn't. The attorney was just some friend. He's okay now. I told him he has me to talk to."

"You know, you didn't grow up with money, so you aren't used to thinking like this, but you have to protect yourself. People are out to get whatever they can from you. It doesn't matter what kind of case they may have, they can sue."

"You sound like your father."

"He could try to sue you for damages if he loses his license. I can hear it now. Sexy little blonde seduces male nurse into murdering her father. Think about it."

"I wish I didn't have money so I didn't have to think that way."

Seth laughed.

"I don't want anything in my name," I said.

"Doesn't matter. They'll come after me."

"Then I don't want to be married anymore, if what I do hurts you. Oh Seth, I wish you could have helped me."

"I couldn't."

"Well then couldn't you have at least let me talk to you about it?"

"I couldn't." Seth looked at me sadly.

"I'm like the lion who had a thorn in its paw," I went on after a while. "He removed it. It's not from the Bible? Some fable?"

"What are you talking about?"

"The male nightnurse. I think he's a good man, simple in a way, but smart. I really believe it. He remembers every word I say. He questions every word I say."

"What did he do exactly? Didn't you give your father the fatal dose?"

"No, it didn't work."

"Did you actually see him mix anything?"

"No."

"Then how do you know?"

"I don't."

"Good. That's what you'll say if anyone asks. Something

doesn't sound right. He is a professional nurse, right? I can't believe a nurse would have trouble overdosing someone."

"He said Dad had fighter's syndrome."

"He probably pretended to give him drugs so that he could get something from you."

"I don't think so."

"He sounds like a predator."

"Not everyone is after money, Seth. He wants *me*, if anything. He wants me to give him credit for what he did."

The phone rang. I answered it quickly.

"Hey," said Thomas. "Give me your number in New York."

"I can't."

"Your husband there?"

"Yes."

"I knew you would change when he showed up."

"I have not changed."

"Are you afraid I'm going to hurt you? Because I'm not."

"My husband is."

"Damn! That pisses me off. What did he say?"

"He thinks you're a predator, that you'll try to blackmail me."

Seth glanced up, realizing who was on the line. "Don't make him mad," he whispered.

"So why are you talking to me?" asked Thomas. "Damage control?"

"I think you want what you did acknowledged."

"Yeah," he said. "Bet you didn't know I got you on video tape, did you? Damn straight. I got some good shots." Thomas laughed, a vulgar sexy laugh. "What do you think about that?"

"I think the world is fucked up, and I don't want to live in it anymore."

"Hey, I'm just playing with you. That really worries you, doesn't it?"

"Yes."

"Well it should."

"What do you want?"

"I just want to be able to see you once a week. There's nothing to keep me in Dallas. Hal, I don't have anything. I can get work in New York. There are lots of rich dudes up there with AIDS that would love to have me as a private nurse. Seth doesn't have to know about it. I don't want to break you up," he went on tiredly. "I just want my time with you, that's all. I don't need much. You've got to cut for me, girl."

When I had hung up Seth asked, "What do you think you're doing?"

"I owe him. He could lose his license. To tell you the truth, I wish he hadn't volunteered. I didn't know it was going to mean so much to him."

"He must face death every day. I don't think you need to worry about *his* emotional well-being. Why isn't he worried about *you*? He must know something about bereaved daughters. He must know that he shouldn't ask anything of you at this point, the day after your father died. I've been here for two hours and you haven't mentioned your father once."

I put my hand over my mouth in horror.

"You've been nursing the nurse."

Dad had said, *Who is this guy? Get him out of here.*

The phone rang, but we didn't answer.

"Why is he calling?" asked Seth. "I thought you said you had resolved everything with him?"

"I don't know!"

"What do you know about this guy? He could be a con artist. He ever go to jail? Do you know?"

"When he was young he was in prison for fraud . . . ."

Seth glared at me. The phone continued to ring. *It would not stop ringing.*

"I'm getting you out of here. Get your bags."

184

XXXII

GHOST OF TELOS. *A rule of faith is what is sought, a semi-flexible, semi-transparent, semi-bright principle to call attention to the pretty tendency, common to many things, to find a pattern of narrower range than one should expect. How should it be possible? and how could we possibly resist temptation to explain? And so a hundred theories meet upon the plain, emblazoned, fitted, polished, and tweaked, and fight until another millennium's gone.*

From the perspective of the sea, the river has purpose. For me my heart has a function, and yet I cannot say that the function of my heart is to pump blood, not even to allow my survival, nor to announce my reproductive fitness. The heart pumps. Blood courses. That's all. Luck and time.

And yet there is perspective. A seer and a thing seen and another believed. Surely there is a place for teleology, a teleology that is not just rhetorical, a mere metaphor that sometimes goes literal in the bush, but telos that is naturalistic and fine, non-normative even in its grandeur, and soft-spoken in a non-mysterious way.

Its place is: in the thing made, by the one who looks forward and back. The artifact, the poem, the woman walking to the market to buy fennel and pears for their perfume and sweetness. And because she walked down to the market, though the day was hot and her time was her own, the man for whom she made the dish thought there was something else in it, some word, some sign of devotion and intent.

People often do things for reasons. For all our cupidity we have aims. And so I like to think there's a reason for that, for my reasoning, my being. And there is, in a sense, in the sense of the whole, in the sense of children, who, trying on titles, will don their own fathers' brushed and laundered names.

My father, David Halperin MacDonald, died on Thanksgiving Day, November 26, 1998 in Dallas, Texas. He was named after his uncle David Halperin MacDonald of Scotland and India who died on November 26, 1948. Annie found a photograph of the eerie tombstone among Dad's things.

A coincidental death date. A telic center into which all my efforts flowed to spite me. So now everyone will accept the tragedy that his death happened to wait till Thanksgiving, November 26th. Now they all can say it was meant to be. Now they can explain why my efforts didn't work.

But what purpose does this double pattern serve? Is it merely for the sake of illustrating divine caprice? *God says when.*

He happened to die on the holiday, and the day happened to be the deathday of his namesake. A phenomenal pattern, unlikely yes, but meaningful? No cause could link the events. Weathermen might argue that the chaos of heaven and ocean has infinite dimensions; therefore, such coincidences are so unlikely as to be unthinkable. I—sitting here alone in my office—know, feel, but cannot prove that my chaos follows a low-dimensional strange path. Yes, there are more possibilities for disorder than for order. But the deck is worn now, and the game can no longer be called fair. It bears a trace. Every day is not equal.

My family was sickened that I left so suddenly before the wake, but they said they understood that I probably needed to get back to work. I sat at my desk doing nothing. Seth was at his studio. *His absence, my palpable sadness.*

Seth had scooped me up in Texas. He had us on a plane to New York within three hours. He was holding my hand and looking forward, and he thought he was helping me leave all of it behind. But when we'd gotten home, he watched me sit on the edge of the bed and smoke a cigarette, and he realized the damage had already been done. I looked up, exhaled. Too late. He saw it. He should have come sooner.

Annie called to say that Thomas had left a message on Candice's answering machine. She played it for me to hear. "What is up? Now, c'mon Hal. You've got that pager number. Use it!"

I took out the paper that had Thomas's pager number written in his school-girlish hand. I called it, punched my number, and waited. *Thomas would not give up responsibility for his actions, even if it meant admitting it took a health professional eight days to beat the metabolism of a sick old man.* The phone rang.

"Yeah. Did someone page me?"

"It's Hali."

"I'm on my way."

I wanted to say yes.

He said, "That's what you want, isn't it? I know I've got you, for whatever reason."

"I need time to think. I need to snap out of it. My oral exams are this week."

"Snap out of what?"

"Death."

"You know what I think is wrong with you? You just wanted to prove to everyone and to yourself that you couldn't do what your father asked of you. Well, guess what. You haven't fooled anybody. You are capable. Your father knew it, and that's why he picked you. Knew you would get the job done."

"But I didn't. I made of mess of it."

"You got me to do it."

I felt my ears were turning red and my head started to swim.

"Hal, you still there? Hal?"

I didn't answer.

"Hal," he said, "I'm sorry. What is it? Say something."

"Seth thinks it's an addiction, you and me. He thinks it's perverse."

"Do you know what it's like for me now? You've got to send me some money to get out of Dallas. I had to work with an oncology patient last night, and I couldn't get Dave MacDonald out of my head. He's on top of me, Hal. He really is."

"I'd rather believe he starved to death. It had been eight days."

"I hate it when you say that, Hal. I did it. I fucking did it. The day before he died, he opened his eyes, Hal, and he looked at me. He looked at me. I still see that man's eyes looking at me. I can't nurse anymore. I can't. I want to talk to someone about it, but my fucking friends tell me to get down on my knees and pray. They're crazy."

"I know how you feel."

"You're the only one."

"Come."

"I'm there, girl."

"It will end badly."

"I know," he said.

"Tommy," I said after a while, "I spoke to Annie. She was going through some of my dad's things and found a picture of his uncle's tombstone. They had the same name, David Halperin MacDonald. And they both died on November 26th."

"Do you know what it means?" replied Thomas. "It means they both died on the same damned day. That's what it means."

And the use you make of it, the effect it has.

* * *

"You have to believe in something. Even if it's only the Big Boom."

* * *

"I dreamt you would ask for my help, Hal. Now what's up with that?"

188

Snow had taken over the TV screen, and Dad was rousing himself, having almost fallen asleep during the final act. "Dad, did I tell you about the article on *Hamlet* that I'm writing?"

"I think you mentioned something. Is that the one where you prove Shakespeare is Hamlet's father?"

"That's James Joyce," I said laughing.

"Oh right."

"I'm writing about a funny coincidence in the play, the way four words form a strange pattern, a hint that should have told Hamlet what to do. It's my idea that if Hamlet had interpreted it as a providential warning, he would have known not to follow the ghost's demand; he would not have been killed, and the fateful Fortinbras would not have been able to take over the kingdom."

"You wouldn't have much of a story then."

"It's as much a story to decide not to act as to decide to act."

"You don't think it was right to listen to his father's ghost?"

"I don't think he should have believed in the ghost."

"But he should have believed that some crazy coincidence was a sign from God? I hate to say this, but that sounds like your mother."

"It sounds like poetry, to me."

Dad climbed out of his chair and ejected the videotape. "That was a good version," he said. "I'm glad you talked me into it. Hey, it's nice having you around, kid." He tied the belt of his robe into a knot above his large belly. He stood there, as if he had something to say. *I wasn't such a mean old man, was I?* There were rare tears in his eyes, and he let me see them. "I'm going to get to bed. See you in the morning."

"Goodnight, Dad. See you in the morning." *Tomorrow you and I will walk the dog. The leaves are turning, and the weather will be fine.*